THE KILLING GROUNDS

"The discovery and death of a serial killer brings the unspoken dramas of an outside-of-the-law small town into focus in this intricate but efficient horror novella ... There's just as much gore and death as horror readers will expect, though it's never gratuitous, and Tierney makes a great and successful effort to equally depict the complex relationships between Bina and her family. By balancing the emotionally resonant with the frightening and bloody, this bite-size tale packs an outsize punch."
—Publishers Weekly (Starred Review)

"A thrilling read. If you like Elizabeth Hand, you'll love Joan Tierney."
—E. Catherine Tobler, author of *The Necessity of Stars*

"I could not put this book down. *The Killing Grounds* is a scintillating story of murder, family, and coming home again. You'll be shocked, saddened, and horrified along the way."
—Eboni Dunbar, author of *Stone and Steel*

"A gritty, suffocatingly immersive small town tale about the bloody shrapnel that remains after the murderer's come and gone—a brilliant and haunting read."
—Anya Ow, author of *Cradle and Grave* and *Ion Curtain*

"Horrifying, heartbreaking and deeply moving all at once, *The Killing Grounds* will keep readers turning the pages. The plot is dark and gripping, the characters are complex and authentic, and the writing is compelling and smooth. I look forward to more from Joan Tierney."
—Lori Duffy Foster, author of the Lisa Jamison Mystery series

Neon Hemlock Press
www.neonhemlock.com
@neonhemlock

The Killing Grounds
Joan Tierney

Cover Photograph by Tema Stauffer
Cover/Interior Design by dave ring
Edited by dave ring

Print ISBN-13: 978-1-952086-57-1
Ebook ISBN-13: 978-1-952086-64-9

Joan Tierney
THE KILLING GROUNDS

Neon Hemlock Press

THE 2023 NEON HEMLOCK NOVELLA SERIES

The Killing Grounds

BY JOAN TIERNEY

To my family—my Dad, my Zed, my Mom, and my Abby: I love you.
Sorry for putting you in this book.

I WAS ON the truck when it happened. We weren't supposed to call them trucks anymore, but that's what they were. The people upstairs wanted us to call them *luxury travel cars*, like maybe if they slapped enough paint over the walls, no one will realize they're just thin sheets of metal. Ever since the decommercialization of regional air travel, more and more autolines had been cropping up all over the States. They came in all sizes these days, but ours could seat eighteen passengers comfortably. As comfortable as you can be, crammed in a semi for long hours at a time, barreling down the interstate. Eighteen people who couldn't afford a chartered airline contract, but were too good for a greyhound. My autoline was based out of Baltimore, St. Louis and Buffalo, working routes throughout the Northeast and Midatlantic. We served the standard refreshments: Dr. Brown's; Cheerwine; Canada Dry, among others. A few light beers and IPA's if you've got the extra cash. Some miniature bottles of Jim Beam and Tito's for the big spenders. Beef jerky, kettle chips and trail mix. All stacked in metal coolers lined along the front wall, with a curtain draped from the ceiling to deliver some semblance of a barrier between the passengers and me, the help. In the far-right corner sat a small kit closet that housed a cassette toilet which got emptied and rinsed out at every stop. For safety concerns, two windows were typically installed per trailer: one on the side and one in the front, behind the curtain, that lined up with an escape hatch at the back of the truck's cab. Usually only the front window was ever used, to pass food and drinks up to the drivers. I also had a fire extinguisher, crash axe, and box of life vests to use in case of a real emergency. I've never had to use them before, but they seemed to give passengers a bit of added comfort. I didn't have the heart to tell them that if the trailer were to actually roll into the water or catch fire, we probably wouldn't be alive to use them anyhow.

The autoline industry was still new enough that most people didn't quite know how it worked. They thought we drove straight through, from departure to arrival depot, but that wasn't true. We made plenty of stops along the way; one trip usually takes a few days. We stayed at a motel in a different city every night—usually nothing fancy, just a boxy room with a busted radiator and a rust-colored carpet—and we pulled over at a rest stop twice each day. People thought the crew paid for our own motel rooms, but the autoline took care of that. They gave the drivers a thick black credit card for gas.

That trip was almost over: St. Louis to Buffalo, and boy were we ready to be done. The route hadn't been very scenic, just long gray stretches of pavement and metal signs signaling Econo Lodges and Taco Bells. The passengers mostly slept and kept to themselves, tucked into their carpet seats. Dan and Craig, the drivers, had worked with me before. We got along, were friends even. Dan and I had met Craig's wife and daughter. They'd both met my roommate during stays in Baltimore. Dan had a house

in Buffalo and had invited us to stay a few nights while
he showed us the city. We'd have three days off before we
were to pick up the trailer and take it to Pittsburgh, just
one afternoon's drive. St. Louis to Buffalo is a three-day
trip. Anything over six hundred miles is automatically
three days. Too many cases of drivers falling asleep at the
wheel, otherwise. We spent the first night in Indianapolis,
then Cleveland. The morning of the third day is when we
picked up the Southern Tier Strangler.

He was waiting for us when we got to the hangar.
Had all the required credentials. He was a driver for a
neighboring company, which meant he didn't have to pay
for a passenger seat and could just ride in the cab if Dan
and Craig had the room. My drivers are nice guys: polite,
always-say-yes types. We made small talk as the passengers
straggled out of the hotel, yawning and sipping at foam
cups of complimentary coffee.

"You live in Buffalo?" Dan asked, drinking from a travel
cup. He makes his own coffee, carrying a bag of grounds
and a silicone pour-over everywhere he goes.

"Nah, haven't lived upstate in years. I'm from some south
of there," said Robert Williams, the name he'd given. "Tiny
little town in Southern Tier. You'd miss it if you blinked."

"What town?" I asked, perking up. Dan had graciously
filled my travel cup too, but I can't drink anything piping
hot, so I was mostly just warming my hands with it. "My
dad's from Southern Tier."

Robert Williams suddenly leaned crooked. That was the
first oddity that I noticed—almost as if he'd been knocked
out of alignment with gravity. He looked at me and rubbed
a hand at the hair on his pale jaw, a tick I'd grown up
watching the men from my father's hometown perform.
"Archer," he said. "Like I said, 's tiny. No one knows it."

"I know it," I told him. "That's where my dad's from.
He's got a house there now. Maybe you know him. Jacob
Morton?"

He bent again, as if battered by wind. Itched his jaw. He looked about my father's age, and Archer really *was* a small town, with just one school shared between them and the hamlet next door. "Doesn't ring a bell," said Robert Williams.

That was the second oddity. Even if he didn't remember my dad, you can't stop anywhere in Archer without hearing the name Morton. My grandfather was a pillar of that town, back when that sort of thing mattered. He was there for every barn raising, helped put out every fire, participated in every function. Before dying of pancreatic cancer at sixty-three, he was a real go-getter. Couldn't seem to go get himself checked by a doctor, but that was just rural living. Anything that couldn't be fixed by milk of magnesia was simply the hand of G-d coming to collect you.

"Well, we don't have any seats open in the back but you're welcome to ride up front," Dan offered.

"Much obliged," said Robert Williams. His teeth were off-white and skinny, overlapping each other when he grinned. "I only needed to catch this ride because my own trip cancelled, but now I'm sorta glad for it. Oats pour when water rises."

Craig shot me a look that said exactly what *he* thought about odd country idioms, and then circled around to the other side of the cab.

I can't tell you why I decided in that moment that something was wrong with Robert Williams. Maybe it was the fact that he kept looking at me from the corner of his eye, as though afraid to face me straight on. Maybe it was the way he kept leaning, as if one small push would knock him over. Maybe it was that he claimed not to recognize my family's name. Probably it was a collection of things. Call it intuition if you like. Mostly it was uncomfortable, like when you're laying in the dark and *know* that you're alone, but you can still feel eyes on you.

My mother used to say that feeling was just our dead loved ones watching over us. She was real fond of ghosts, my mother. They were the answer for anything she couldn't outright explain. Plus I think she liked the idea that nothing was ever really over. That existence might be open ended.

Once the boys were all situated in the cab—not so cramped that they'd be uncomfortable, but not particularly spacious either—I sent a message to my father. He doesn't have a cell phone, because he doesn't trust whatever corporation is listening from the other side. He likes technology, my dad, but he likes it on his terms. Instead he has a tablet with an encrypted VPN, which he'd set up to receive messages like a two-way pager.

I messaged him: *Picked up a guy in Cleveland, says he's from Archer. Robert Williams. You know him?*

He doesn't tend to respond quickly, so I slipped my phone back in my bag behind the curtain and focused on getting the passengers settled in for the day. My dad had been living alone with my niece ever since my brother got locked up in Monroe County three years earlier. That made my niece, Abby, nine now. I'd moved to Baltimore a year after Abby was born and she'd been a toddler the last time I'd gone to Archer. She'd mostly just sat on my brother's lap and gazed up at me with brown eyes, round as a calf's. She probably didn't remember me. She probably barely remembered her parents.

We were just outside Rochester's city limits when I thought to check my phone again. We'd made good time, but it was still nearly sundown and we had another hour-and-change to go. To my surprise, my dad's message had arrived just after I'd sent mine.

It said: *Don't be alone with him.*

The thing about my dad is, for all his house could be mistaken for a doomsday prepper's, he's the most trusting guy I've ever known. He'll pick up a hitchhiker,

no questions asked, and drive him over state lines just to
help him out. When Zed first called from the jailhouse,
telling Dad how Liza was dead and the cops thought
it was his fault, Dad didn't hesitate to believe in his
innocence. He hadn't hesitated a year earlier when it was
Liza on the other line either, arrested for blowing a 2.0
on a breathalyzer, after she'd wrapped the car around a
telephone pole with baby Abby in the backseat, swearing
to him up and down that she'd quit drinking. My dad likes
to see the best side of people, even if a best side isn't there.

So there I am, the most trusting man in the universe
warning me about the stranger currently sandwiched
between two of my friends. I opened up a new message to
Craig, since I knew Dan was driving that leg.

I told him: *My dad said this jumpseater is shady. Be careful.*

Less than a minute later, Craig sent back: *Rgr.*

I don't know what happened in those next six minutes.
I think it was six minutes. It might have been less. People
always say, when tragedy strikes, that the event itself
"happened so fast," and they can't remember much of
anything. I didn't understand that before, not really. I knew
the theory. Like learning about Newton's first law of motion.
An object in motion tends to stay in motion. Sure, that makes
sense. You get the truth of it, objectively. But you don't fully
understand it until you experience it. When you're in a truck,
going seventy miles an hour down the interstate and then
suddenly the trailer starts to swerve dangerously. And in the
cab, the driver hits the brakes but it's too late, because the
trailer was already in motion. And in that moment, all you
can think about is that forty-five minute lesson from twelfth
grade physics, and you think, *I get it now.*

I do remember bits and pieces from immediately before
and after the crash itself. The sharp swerve was first,
just minutes after I got Craig's text. I cried out for the
passengers to buckle their seatbelts and strapped into my
own jumpseat. I remember the gunshot next. There was

just the one. Craig and Dan both carried a .45 ACP in their side holsters. I didn't know if Robert Williams had a gun. If he did, he was obligated to tell the crew he was riding with, but that didn't mean he would have.

After the gunshot, the swerving picked up in earnest. Then the brakes. As the trailer tipped, I felt it happen slowly, though I know it must have been fast. The passengers were screaming and crying. The smell of piss soured the air. Luggage and snacks were flung through the cabin. The landing's impact sent a brittle shock of vibrations through my body; my teeth clacked painfully, two of them chipping, but otherwise I was intact.

I carry a pocket knife for my own safety, which I used to cut through the straps of my jumpseat, disinterested in battling the buckles for release. The trailer was about eight feet wide inside, but the coolers had helpfully stacked themselves in the fall, so I could swing my legs around and perch atop the makeshift stool. There, I could reach the window that faced the back of the cab and pry it open. The cab itself had managed to stay right side up in the melee—I don't know how. It went beyond what I remembered of physics. The cab's back window, facing me, was smeared with blood and impossible to see through. The trailer was several feet away, detached from the fifth wheel.

I called Dan and Craig's names but got no response. I heaved myself through the window, dropping to the soggy earth outside. I jogged over to the cab, reaching the driver's side as the door was wrenched open. Dan fell to the ground, skin and clothes bloody. It took me a minute to realize he wasn't hurt.

"Craig," I gasped, but Dan shook his head, wincing from the movement.

"He's okay," he told me. "We're okay. That bastard—" he cut himself off and swore. From the other side of the cab, I heard the door open and Craig drop to the ground himself, crossing around to us. He was even bloodier than Dan. Clots of dark matter soaked through his shirt and the brown skin of his neck. There was no way someone could survive that kind of blood loss. I looked back up at the cab.

"Don't," said Dan, shepherding me away. "Go look after the passengers. I'll call the cops."

The trailer had tipped at an angle that allowed me to open the back door, rolling it up from the side. Inside the cabin, people had skittishly released themselves from their seats and slid down to the makeshift floor. No one seemed too grievously injured, though a few were still stuck under jammed seat belts that had to be cut through. I got everyone outside and sat them down, shaking, against the ruined guard rail. It wasn't too cold out, but a few of us collected every blanket we could find, draping them over everyone's shoulders for a little comfort. More than a few pilfered the liquor coolers and froze when I caught their eye, but I turned away.

"What, exactly, happened?" I asked Dan, once I'd seen to the passengers. He and Craig sat drooping in front of the cab, waiting for the police to arrive.

"After I got your text, I started to ask him some questions," said Craig. He spoke loudly, ears clearly still ringing from the gunshot. His voice was hoarse and nasally, on account of Robert Williams having broken his nose. I fetched some tampons from my purse, so he could staunch the blood. "I thought I was being discreet, but I guess he cottoned on. Then he elbowed me in the face, and tried to pull Dan's gun."

"So you shot him?" I asked. Craig was just a year older than me, and had been a television repairman before he got hired by our autoline. As far as I knew, he'd never shot anyone before.

He didn't answer. Dan said, "He did what he had to do." Dan had been in a motorcycle gang in his early twenties.

"Of course," I agreed. We flanked Craig protectively as the sound of sirens approached.

Robert Williams' body was still inside the cab. Two of the officers set about taking photographs and swabbing blood. The others began taking statements. They started with my drivers and me first, since the passengers had been in the trailer for most of it. It took six vehicles to cart everyone to the police station, groups of three or four in the backs of cruisers and F250s. Rochester had a well-funded station, with real chairs in the lobby and shiny new computers on every desk. As with any other private business, you could tell which stations were well-off and cared for, and which ones were just a bunch of badge jockeys scraping by for the tax cuts.

Archer didn't have a police department. They never have. They couldn't afford to charter one, and they didn't see the need to petition for one appointed by the state. And corporate America had no interest in sponsoring a tiny farm town that hadn't seen much in the way of financial success since the dairy industry's slow collapse. The more rural counties in Southern Tier were badge-less, running mostly on the logic that as every household carries at least one gun, and there wasn't much stopping someone from seeking retribution as they see fit, it'd be relatively stupid to provoke them. For the most part, it worked. The worst crime places like Archer sees were hunting without proper tags, and no one much cares about that.

The officer taking my statement, whose last name was Penn, seemed to understand. "I've got an uncle in Belmont," he said. "I know about the mountain law. You say this man Robert Williams was from there?"

"Archer, he said. He claimed not to recognize my dad's name, but my dad sure knew his."

"Any idea why he'd try a stunt like this?" Penn asked. "Why not just get off at the next pitstop, if he was so worried about his privacy?"

"I don't know," I said. "I'm not a detective. I didn't even know the guy."

"Seems a bit suicidal," said Penn.

"Maybe he wanted to die," I suggested. "Maybe he wanted to take everyone else out with him. Wouldn't be the first time a man snapped like that."

"Hum," said Penn. "Thank you, Ms. Morton. Is this a good number to contact you for any further questions we may have?" He parroted my phone number back at me and I nodded. "And you have a place to stay?"

"My dad's place is just over an hour from here."

Penn looked at me from over the rim of his glasses. "You okay to drive?"

"He's picking me up," I lied. I hadn't actually called him yet, but I didn't have it in me to sit there and take advice from some baby-faced cop convinced I had PTSD.

I found Dan and Craig sitting on a bench by the payphone. I sank down in the space between them.

"I called the autoline," Dan said. "They're giving us paid time off while we *process*. And they're sending someone to collect the truck."

"Isn't it evidence?"

Dan shrugged. "I imagine the autoline will have to pay a pretty penny, but every badge has his price. Some cash will probably 'expedite the process.'"

"Are you still heading to Buffalo?" I asked. He could probably rent a car and make it there in under two hours, but I wasn't sure how eager he was to get behind another wheel. He looked ready to collapse, even though he was already sitting.

"I don't know," he admitted. "I might get a room here for the night and see how I feel in the morning."

Craig lived in St. Louis. He still looked relatively shell-shocked. The tampons I'd given him had been replaced with professional gauze and bandages. I didn't like the thought of leaving him alone.

"I'm gonna call my dad to come get me. He lives near here. You guys can stay with us if you want. Just until you feel up for the road again," I offered. It was, I knew, rude to offer them the guest bed before talking it over with my dad first. I did it anyway. At their hesitation, I added, "He's already got to make the drive, to get me. You might as well tag along. That way you don't have to worry about the motel reimbursement paperwork."

"Alright," Dan conceded. Craig gave a slight tilt of his head, which I took as affirmation.

I called my dad. It was late enough to be in the *bad timeframe*, that collection of hours during which he says a phone call always means bad news. He'd gotten the call from my mother around this time and then, years later, the calls from Liza and Zed.

He answered on the fourth ring. "Bee?" He sounded wary and each of his sixty-three years, stretched thin and taut like a thread liable to snap. I wondered if he thought I'd been arrested, like my brother and sister-in-law, or if this call would be more like my mom's.

"Hey, dad. I'm in Rochester. There's been a situation." I summarized the evening for him. "The autoline's giving us some time off. Can you come get us?"

"Us?"

"Me and my drivers. They need a place to stay for the night."

"Just for the night?"

"Maybe more." I could hear his mouth moving like a cow at its own cud, a leftover from when he used to chew tobacco. "They're good guys. We're all a little shook up."

"Course," my dad said. "Give me an hour 'n some."

"You need the address?" He did, so I asked the receptionist and then echoed it over to him.

"So Rob's dead, then?"

At the sound of his name, my mind pulled up the image of his blood all over the cab windows, staining Craig and Dan's shirts, caught in the creases of their skin.

"Yep," I assured him. "Dead as the Devil." We hung up, and I called my roommate back in Baltimore, a lesbian named Miranda who bartended at a go-go bar. I gave her the bare bones of the story and asked her to water my plants, the closest thing to a pet my work would ever allow me.

"I knew your job was interesting but I didn't think it was *that* kind of interesting." Miranda whistled. "Hijackers are on *lounge trailers*, now? Are you sure you're okay? Want me to come get you?"

"You work tonight," I pointed out, biting back a smile. It was a nice offer.

"Patrick can screw off," Miranda said blithely. "I'll take a sick day. If Oslow can take one every time he gets his asshole bleached, then I can definitely take one when my roommate almost *dies*."

"I'm fine. My dad's coming to get me and the guys. I'll probably stay with him for a while."

"Alright," Miranda said, sounding unconvinced. "But if you need a ride back to civilization, just say the word."

Craig's phone was dead and he'd misplaced his charger, so he used mine to call his wife and daughter. Dan and I sat in companionable silence. I didn't know where the passengers had gone after giving their own statements. Hopefully the autoline had put everyone up in a local hotel, but I wasn't sure company policy covered this sort of thing.

Craig came back half an hour later and handed my phone back without a word.

"Did you tell them what happened?" I asked.

"Some," he said, and the silence resumed.

My dad came in through the front door sometime later. His beard was longer and grayer than it had been the last time I'd seen him, but he was otherwise unchanged. I'd changed a lot, but he still seemed to recognize me.

"Your hair's long," he commented. It was also dark, thanks to a drunken night at Miranda's bar and a box of black dye someone had left behind in the bathroom.

When he'd last seen me, I'd only had a thin layer of peach fuzz, freshly shaved.

"So's your beard," I said. "Dad, this is Dan and this is Craig. Guys, this is my dad." The three shared a round of sober nods.

"Well, come on then," said my dad. "We're burning daylight." He led us out to the ancient Jeep Cherokee, freckled with rust and mud that was older than me.

"I can't believe she's still running," I said, swinging myself into the front seat.

In the back, wrapped up in a quilt and buckled into the center seat, was Abby. She blinked out at me fuzzily, eyes bleary with sleep but still just as round and chocolate-brown as I remembered. I turned back towards the road without a word.

"Who's this?" Craig asked kindly. His own daughter was around Abby's age.

"That's Abby," said my dad. He offered no further explanation and neither did I. The radio ground out an old Emmylou Harris tune as we drove.

Each mile felt like a blink. There were seven tolls between Rochester and Archer. The last two belonged to the electric company that powered all of southwestern New York. My dad had me fish his membership license from the glovebox; since he paid them every month to keep the lights on, he got a discount on the tolls. We could tell immediately when we left sponsored country. The smooth pavement of highway turned into dirt, the grass on either side untrimmed and flushed with goldenrod. Pebbles kicked up against the Jeep's undercarriage as we drove through the dust. My dad's old house was the only light for miles, since Aunt Bethany's trailer across the street was obscured by maple and hemlock trees. On the house's other side stood an abandoned Presbyterian church and an old cemetery filled with Union soldiers. I felt nearly too tired to lift my hand and open the door.

In the backseat, Abby and Craig had fallen asleep completely. Dan had to wake them up.

The house was almost exactly as I remembered it, which wasn't as comforting as it might have been if I'd ever considered it home. I ran my fingers over my dad's collection of field notes and bird guides, less dusty than the rest of the stuff on the cluttered shelves. My mother had been the decorator, always concerned with the way things looked in a way my dad never was. He carried Abby upstairs, still bundled up and head lolling. I set up the sofa bed for Dan and Craig, who assured me they were just fine with sharing. I showed them where the bathroom was, and how to work the water filter.

"Don't just drink it from the tap," I warned them. "There's too much sulfur in the soil here. It won't taste right."

"We'll survive," Dan said, shooing me towards the stairs. "Get some sleep."

The part I'd been avoiding; being left with what had once been my childhood bedroom, the wooden D still hung up on the door. It was different, of course, filled with old furniture and milk crates that wouldn't fit anywhere else. The walls were still the baby pink of my younger years, with scraps of song lyrics and poetry scribbled in patches by my teenaged hands. My dad had never yelled at me over it. I think he liked the show of personality. My mom was the only one who would have cared, and she was already long gone by then.

Across the room, an old tomato can, emptied and washed out, sat atop my dresser. A small bit of yarn had been tied through the hole drilled into the can's bottom. A second matching can was buried outside. I had crafted this crude telephone when I was nine, the summer my mother left. I'd been convinced she had become one of her ghosts, and so I would need a different way to communicate with her. In my childish mind, ghosts lived in the earth, and so that was where I needed to direct my messages. I called her every night that summer, chattering on about my day, waiting for her to respond. It took me a stupidly long time to realize she was never going to. Longer to realize she probably wasn't even dead. It simply had never occurred to me that a mother might leave her children for any other reason.

The bed felt small now, my feet hanging over the edge when I laid down arrow-straight. Above my head was scrawled a line from *Julius Caesar*, which I'd fallen in love with my sophomore year: "Cry havoc and let slip the dogs of war." It was a macabre image to fall asleep to, but I'd been a macabre thing those motherless years.

In the morning, I descended the stairs as if I was heading into the Underworld. Melodramatic, but this town had always brought that out in me. Growing up in a small town was a prison sentence. Every day, the same faces, the same things to do, desperately trying to pass the time. In Archer, everyone lived like they were checking boxes off a list of things they had to do before they could die. Death was a relief. Finally, they're free of it all.

In the living room, the mattress had been folded back into the sofa, and Abby was seated at the coffee table with a coloring book. She was plucking bits of dry cereal out of a bowl, eating mechanically while she drew. Her eyes fell on me like a weighted net.

"Good morning," I said, feeling trapped by the vague attention of a nine-year-old. Children's minds were always skipping, I reminded myself, like flat rocks over water, quick to change focus. She would soon lose interest in me, and I could drift throughout the house unnoticed, safe as a ghost.

"Grandpa says you're here because a bad man tried to hurt you," Abby said without preamble.

"He's right," I admitted. "But I'm okay."

"Is the bad man okay?" she asked, and I floundered.

"No."

Unaffected, Abby turned her attention back to the coloring book. "Grandpa says you're my aunt, like Aunt Bethany."

"Actually, Aunt Bethany is *my* aunt, because she's your grandpa's sister. Your grandpa is my dad. I'm your daddy's sister."

Abby made a face. "Then what's Aunt Bethany?"

"She's your great aunt."

She looked unimpressed by this minor detail. "My daddy's in jail," she told me. "Have you ever been to jail?"

"Once. Not as long as your daddy, though."

"Grandpa says jail isn't always for bad guys. Sometimes it's for people who make mistakes and need time to fix them."

"Your grandpa sounds like a very smart man," said Dan, who I hadn't heard sneaking up behind me. He passed me a cup of coffee. "Your dad made breakfast."

"Let me guess; scrambled eggs." It was the one thing he could reliably cook. That and spaghetti.

"They're good." Dan smiled. "Well-seasoned."

In the kitchen, I found Craig eating his own eggs at the bar countertop, two more plates steaming next to him. My dad was rinsing out his coffee grinder. He doesn't allow himself a lot of luxuries, my dad, but coffee's his one vice. He likes the good stuff, and drives an hour out of his way to get it. He grinds his own beans and then makes it with a French press. When I was in high school, he used to put brown sugar around the rim of my mug and leave it on the nightstand for me to wake up to. He never said much, but I could never accuse him of not caring.

We were just finishing up breakfast when my cousins showed up, stomping in with their mired muck boots and camo-print sweatshirts. My cousins—David, Becky and Benji—always traveled together, like mud-covered pack animals. They each gave me a perfunctory, bear-armed hug before congregating around the table. I introduced them to my drivers. They nodded gruffly, eyeing the sleeves of ink on Dan's pale skin, shooting Craig surreptitious looks from under their eyelashes. Abby came scuttling in from the living room and perched herself on David's lap as if it was a daily ritual.

"You hear the news, yet?" David asked us.

"What news?" said Dad. "You know I don't have television."

"It was on the radio," said Benji. "Some guy was killed in Rochester. They think he was a serial killer."

I caught Dan and Craig's eyes over the countertop. "A serial killer?"

Benji nodded, swiping a clementine from a bowl on the table. He started to peel the skin off in one long coil with a dirty thumbnail. "I guess his fingerprints were found at a bunch of crime scenes in different cities. Binghamton, Bath, even Hornell."

"Hornell?" Dad frowned.

"That's just forty-five minutes from here," I told my drivers.

"They're calling him the Southern Tier Strangler," said Becky. "Didn't catch his real name."

"I didn't think we were big enough to have a serial killer," added Benji.

"His name was Robert Williams," I said. "He was on our truck to Buffalo last night."

My cousins looked us over appraisingly. "No shit?" asked David. "I'll be damned."

"Two quarters," Abby said primly, scooting off his lap and fetching a mason jar from the curio cabinet across the room. Inside was a small collection of one dollar bills and loose change.

David pulled a crumpled dollar from his back pocket and stuffed it in the jar. "For the rest of the day."

I turned back to my dad. "Where did Robert Williams live?"

"Up near Hickory Crick. Hadn't lived there for years, though. Not since we run him out." He glanced at Abby. "Why don't you go see the kittens."

Abby frowned. "You said I shouldn't bother them."

"You can bother them now," my dad promised. "Their mama won't mind. Just be gentle." She scampered off. At the sound of the screen door slamming shut behind her, his shoulders slumped.

"Who ran him out?" asked Dan. "Why?"

My dad sighed, leaning a hip against the sink, uncaring of the wet soaking through his sweater. "You're from Buffalo?" When Dan nodded, hhe turned to Craig. "And you're from St. Louis. So I'm guessing neither of you ever lived outside the shadow of a badge."

"Bina said Archer doesn't have a police department," Dan said.

At the table, David made a face. "Bina? You mean Debbie?"

"I go by Bina now, Dave," I told him. He made another face.

"Archer never had a police department," said my dad. "Not ever, even before the privatization. And it's a pretty old town, for the States. No hospitals, no police, just a volunteer fire department. People 'round here don't have the money to spend, paying people to take care of us, so we learned to take care of ourselves. We got a couple medics in town, local guys who don't mind house calls."

"But couldn't you apply for a hospital grant?" asked Dan.

"We did, in the seventies. Wasn't worth the cost to build one. There aren't a lot of people out here anyhow, and the ones who are don't trust doctors, or uniforms. Too easy for them to charge us for things we don't need. We got the state-sanctioned county department, but they don't usually poke their noses round here, and we don't give 'em cause to." He glanced at me, and I knew he was thinking about Zed, because I was too. Zed, whose mistake had been wrecking his car in the next county over. "Mostly, that's because we don't get a lot of crime around here. Hunting without tags, maybe some livestock poaching, but that gets sorted out pretty quickly. And that's the other reason. We clean up our own messes."

"And Robert Williams was a mess?" Craig surmised.

"Robert Williams was collateral," Dad corrected. "He lived in a trailer with his dad, out in the woods. Quiet kid, for the most part. There was always something a little off about them, but people 'round here like to leave well enough alone."

"What changed?"

"Three women went missing. In just one year. People leave, you understand. Not often, but it happens. But three of 'em, back to back, all young, pretty, planning their futures. They just vanished. We knew it wasn't right."

"Who were the women?" I asked. "Did you know them?"

"I grew up with them," Dad said darkly. "We all did. Jack Williams, that was Rob's dad, he was the main suspect. Not for all of them, but the last one—Kathy Owens—people saw her get into his car for a ride home in a rainstorm. He said he dropped her off at her daddy's place, but she never showed. So, we knew."

"Owens, like Jeb Owens?" asked David. "The mayor?"

"Retired mayor now," Benji pointed out.

My dad nodded. "Kathy was his sister."

"So you ran them both out of town?" I clarified.

My dad went quiet for a moment. "We looked all over for Kathy and the others. Their trailer, those woods, even raked the crick for four days. Never found one trace of 'em."

"Dad, what did you do with the Williamses?"

"Jack, when we interrogated him, he laughed in our faces. He didn't confess, not in so many words, but he laughed about it. We asked where the girls were, and he said he always fed what's left to the pigs, after he went hunting. We knew there was no saving him, then. But Rob, he was still young. We figured, no point punishing the son for the sins of the father."

"If his dad really did kill those women, he probably knew about it," I pointed out. I thought back to Robert Williams, the lines of his face that seemed to sharpen at the sound of my father's name. The way he'd leaned, as if instinctively trying to evade me. He'd thought I might recognize him. He'd thought I'd know what he was.

"What year was this?" I asked.

My dad met my gaze evenly. "1999."

The year my mother left us. I felt sure I wasn't breathing, but I must have been, because I asked, "What were their names? The other women who went missing."

"Alice and Barbara," my dad said gently. "Your mother called me, Bee. From the motel, remember? There's no reason to think she got caught up in all this."

"The motel in Bath," I said, turning to David. "You said he killed someone in Bath, right?"

"Yeah," David said hesitantly. "But they didn't list any names, or—"

I turned back to my dad. "I want to see where he lived. The trailer in the woods. I want you to show me."

My dad sighed. "Bee—"

"He could have killed me," I snapped. "He almost killed my friends. Hell, he almost killed twenty-one people. He should have been behind *bars*."

"We dealt with him the way we knew how."

"By making him someone else's problem." He ducked from my gaze. I turned to David. "You know where this place is?"

"If it's out near Hickory Crick, I know the area," he admitted. "I dunno about any trailer, though."

"It's not much of anything, anymore," my dad said. "Rusted away without upkeep. Don't do anything stupid like wander off on your own. I'll take you." He sounded tired.

I borrowed my grandmother's old pair of muck boots. People out here like to hoard; you never know what you might need in the future, and you probably won't have the money to buy it. Minimalism was the rich man's interior design.

The earth was soft and wet, despite two days having passed since the last rainstorm. Archer was always wet when I thought of it. Wet and muddy. Most of the land had been depleted by years of overharvesting and then gnawed at by livestock until only oozing pits of sludge and patches of untamed forest remained. The woods were as unwelcoming as the rest of the town. These weren't the kind of trees you went for a leisurely hike in. There were no real trails, for one. Each step was a fight with burdock briars and spiderwebs.

Dad sent Abby over to Aunt Bethany's across the road, supposedly to help her with canning. Then the cousins, the drivers, and I trailed after him up the dirt road towards Hickory Crick. The crick itself wasn't much to write home about—muddy water over a bed of sharp rocks. Zed and I, like every other kid in Archer, used to spend our summers catching tadpoles and, occasionally, silver minnows flickering through our fingers like sewing pins. We'd go home with new cuts on the soles of our feet every night, wincing with each step, until eventually the skin grew thick and calloused.

My feet were softer, now. My hands, too. I scraped my palms on rough tree hide as we climbed through the underbrush, gritting my teeth at the sting of pain. Up ahead, my dad paused on the incline. We huffed up after him.

Just over the ridge sat the corpse of the Williams' trailer. It was an old Airstream, popular in the thirties and forties, once painted bullet-silver. Now it was more rust than anything else, ceiling and walls bowing inwards. Rotting milk crates filled with trash littered the immediate area, spilling through the unhinged door. All manner of animals had migrated to this mecca, making homes out of the moth-eaten sofa and hollow juice cartons. I had very little interest in the trailer itself, now that I saw how debased it was. No way had Robert Williams planned on staying in this.

I glanced inside the unhinged door, finding more mayhem and debris. Just to the left of me sat a stack of old bondage porn magazines, pages crippled by rain. The covers advertised women spread-eagle, covered in ropes and chains, crying from pain or pleasure or both, bleeding from the veins in their naked thighs.

The group of us dispersed, kicking through the junk and decomposing leaves. We were, I thought mildly, trampling evidence. It was likely that, if Robert Williams really *was* a serial killer, the FBI or some other important acronym would want to come out here and collect the pieces of his life for their labs and criminology classes. Probably, they wouldn't be too happy about a bunch of hicks plodding all over what could very well be a crime scene itself.

I continued to plod, catching sight of a rickety lean-to constructed around the back of the trailer. It was still standing, albeit miserably, though I couldn't see a reason for it. There was no riding lawn mower, no dilapidated surge milker, no old car parts to be fiddled with. It wasn't even storing any toolboxes. It was empty, save for the corner of what looked like an old tarp, poking out of the loose soil and leaf litter like an outstretched hand. Gingerly, I scuffed the tarp with my foot, flinging more of it free. Hidden underneath, I saw it: a human foot, bare and dirty.

"Dad," I said, not nearly loud enough. The others weren't beside me, but I couldn't pull my eyes away to search them out. I only stared at the foot and listened to my breathing like the crashing of waves. "Dad," I called again, only a little louder. Without conscious thought, I stooped down and tugged at the tarp, pulling it from the shallow grave completely.

"What'd you find?" David asked, stomping over. He stopped just a few feet behind me, frozen at the sight, same as I was.

The tarp in my hands was only one of many lining the shallow grave. The hole itself held the bodies of five women. Five that I could see. There might've been more buried underneath. They were all naked, all at various levels of decay. One of the bottom ones was mostly bone, with some darkened gummy bits that looked petrified. Half of them had mushrooms sprouting from them, like a macabre garden. The topmost body, whose foot I'd seen, was in the best shape. She couldn't have been dead very long, I thought. Her body wasn't rotted at all yet, despite missing the bottom half of her face.

"Her jaw," I said dumbly. "He took her lower jaw."

Behind me, David turned and vomited. At the sound, the others came skidding around the trailer and approached the lean-to.

"Holy shit," said Dan.

"Becky, run back to your mom's and call the county department," my dad ordered. Becky took off running, boots skidding against the muddy leaves as she went.

"Benji, don't look," Dave coughed, wiping a sleeve against his mouth.

I crouched down to get a better look at the first girl, the one missing her jaw. She was my age, or just about. I held a hand up, blocking the lower half of her face, so I could almost pretend she was intact. With her eyes closed, it just looked like she was sleeping.

"It's Suzette," I realized, remembering the faded image of a pretty blonde girl from my class.

"Don't touch her," Dan warned. "You don't want to mess up any DNA they might be able to pull."

I didn't touch her. There was a line of bruising around her throat, like the candy necklaces we used to wear and eat in class, snapping the hard sugar between our teeth when the teacher wasn't looking. Some of the bruises were still dark, but many of them were the green-yellow that came from healing. I studied them with a frown. Had he buried her alive?

I was still staring at her throat, that's why I saw when it started moving.

Sometimes insects crawled inside dead bodies, I knew. They lived inside them, a little apartment complex for the maggots and blowflies. Probably I was witnessing the movement of a fly who had hatched under her skin. There was no way she could be breathing. She was missing the lower half of her face. She'd been buried under a tarp in the woods for days, at least, if not weeks.

But her throat moved like a throat struggling to work, not like a tunnel being mined by a beetle. Her eyes blinked open—dilated and glazed, but open.

"She's alive," I said, sounding much calmer than I felt. I felt like I was on fire, like I'd been burning for so long that I couldn't tell if I was hot or cold.

"What?" said Craig, leaning closer, even as he clearly longed to run away.

"She's alive," I repeated, reaching for her. I had a split-second fear that I'd touch her, only for her skin to come sloughing off under my hand, proof that she was dead after all.

"Bina—" said Dan.

Suzette's mangled mouth shifted, unsure how to do its job when half of it was missing. The sound she made was not really a scream—she couldn't put that much power behind it. But it was enough. I took her hand, which was cold and wet, but still solid.

"G-d Almighty," said my dad. He gripped Benji by the shoulders. "Go after your sister, tell her to make sure they send an ambulance, tell them—" he looked back at the grave, eyes wide and skittish. "Hell, I don't care *what* you tell 'em. Just get 'em *here*." Benji ran.

In her grave, Suzette was staring out towards the sunlight. She wasn't focusing on anything as far as I could tell. I wasn't even sure she could see. I clutched her hand and leaned in, breathing through my mouth to stave off the stench of rot.

"Suzette," I told her. "It's Deborah Morton, from school. Remember me? Help's coming."

There was no clear reaction that indicated she could hear or understand me. Tears began to leak from the corners of her eyes, which remained strained and open, as if she was afraid to close them again. I kept hold of her hand until we heard the cops approaching, their steps harsh and clumsy in the unfamiliar territory.

One of them vomited too.

The ambulance showed up soon after, and they carried Suzette on a stretcher through the trees. They checked the other women for pulses, just in case, but Suzette was the only survivor.

"How'd you find this place?" one of the officers—his nametag said only the letter T—demanded.

"Everyone 'round here knows about it," my dad shrugged.

"Why were you all out here?"

"We were on the truck with Robert Williams yesterday," I said. "The Southern Tier Strangler. I wanted to see where he used to live. For closure."

Officer T frowned down at me. He was very tall and very broad. To anyone else, he might have seemed imposing. If I'd been up to feeling intimidated, I might have found him imposing too. As it was, I was just tired of having to crane my neck to look him in the eye. "Closure," he said.

"Yeah. Sometimes people want it, after they go through a traumatic event. Sometimes they even act erratically, or out of character."

"Like going looking for a serial killer's den in the middle of the woods," Dan said dryly.

"Maybe," I said.

"Uh-huh," said Officer T. "Alright. I'll need to take down everyone's statements. And your fingerprints, if you touched anything."

"We may have touched some things," I admitted.
Officer T looked unsurprised.

So two evenings in a row I spent wringing my memory
at police stations, their fingers flying over keyboards,
recording every word I said, panning them like stones
in water, hoping one or two might turn out to be gold.
The county station was everything Rochester's was not;
outdated, unsponsored, and unclean. The building itself
was unpainted cement with corrugated ceilings that
looked ready to collapse. County stations almost always
look like that, not much more than a last ditch effort from
the government to have some say in how the county's run,
subsisting on whatever crumbs they manage to wring from
locals' taxes. My interview room was little more than a
cubicle. The interviewing officer grew irritated with me
quickly.

"But *why* did you look in the lean-to? Why not the
trailer, or anywhere else?"

"I don't know," I said, again. "I guess I thought it was
strange that it was empty. Everything else was so cluttered
with junk."

"What made you pull the tarp up?"

"I just did," I said. At his flat stare, I added,
"Sometimes people just do things."

"Like how you *just knew* something was off about Robert
Williams?"

"According to my dad, everyone in town thought
something was off about him."

"But no one ever did anything to stop him."

My eyes slid towards the door that I knew separated
me from my father, who sat on the other side delivering
his own chipped slate of memories. "They made him
leave the town. They had no evidence that he'd done
anything."

"They could have called the county department with
their suspicions."

I looked back at the officer. He'd introduced himself before we began, but I'd already forgotten and he didn't wear a nametag. "Do you really think that would have changed anything?"

"It might have," he insisted, and I think he even believed it. Cops like him have to believe in the system. If they start to look for cracks in the foundation, they won't be able to stop finding them.

"Well, they didn't, and I couldn't," I said. "Seeing as I was nine."

"But you don't remember ever seeing Mr. Williams or his father when you were younger?"

"No. I didn't recognize him, either. I only knew who he was because he told me."

"Why didn't he give you a fake name, do you think?"

"I don't know. Maybe he didn't think I'd ask about him. Or maybe he wanted to be caught."

"You think he wanted to be caught?"

"Well, maybe he was tired of running," I revised. "Don't you think serial killers must get tired? Running and hiding all the time? I bet it takes a lot of energy to kill somebody."

The officer stared at me, hands suspended above his clunky, ancient keyboard. I didn't realize how obnoxious the constant clacking of his fingers against plastic was until it stopped. I blinked back at him. Even my eyelids felt sluggish with exhaustion. If I were a car, my battery light would've clicked on.

"Right. Thank you for your cooperation, Ms. Morton," he said, clearing his throat. "We'll be in touch."

Once again, the group of us piled into my father's Jeep and made the drive back to Archer. No attempt was made at conversation, each of us still wallowing in the muck of our own thoughts. It was the thickest silence I'd ever had to wade through, nearly tangible where it spread out within the car. If I breathed too deeply, it might've seeped into my lungs.

We swung by Aunt Bethany's to pick up Abby, but she'd already brought her home. My father's younger sister had grown up the way most kids in towns like Archer do: young and hard. Most of them are accidents or farmhands at birth. The women are always accidents. I'm not saying they're unloved, but when you have fields to plow, it's sons you want. In Archer, girls are born with the compulsion to prove their worth. They aim to hunt better, plow better, milk better, and drink better. They learn to roll their daddy's cigarettes better. They become the best sons anyone could ask for, and Bethany was no different. She'd dropped out of high school by fifteen, taking over most of the farm work after my dad moved to the city. Then she got in the family way with David and my dad moved back.

Probably that's why Bethany and my dad spoil Abby the way they do. By Abby's age, Bethany was already fetching and herding cattle. But I guess part of being a parent is seeing how your parents fell short, and trying to bridge that gap a little, to ease the way for the next generation. Like laying your jacket over a mud puddle so their boots don't soak through.

Bethany had a twin sister, once. I've seen the baby sketches in the family album. I don't know what happened to her. Around here, you don't talk about the dead. As if by being buried, they've been erased. After a certain amount of time, it's like they never existed.

Abby was curled up like a pillbug on the sofa when we walked in. My dad carried her upstairs without a word, Bethany giving a squeeze to my shoulder on her way out the door. Dan and Craig looked just as lost as they'd been the night before.

"I bet this isn't what you expected when I offered you a place to stay," I joked. Even with the forced lightness, my voice sounded brittle.

"I'm sure it's a nice enough place usually," said Craig.

"You'd be surprised."

"Bina, I'm from St. Louis. I'm no stranger to killings."

"It's different when it's out here," I sighed. "You're taught not to expect it. When I was a kid, everyone always seemed so proud that we didn't have a station, because it meant we didn't have any crime—not like those big cities. But that wasn't true, really. It just meant we were on our own with it."

Dan laid a hand on my arm. "I'll get this set up." He gestured to the sofa, the pile of linens still folded in the corner from the morning. "You go rest."

"I'm fine," I assured him, and willed it to be true. I'd stayed behind as they carried the women out of their hole, one by one, and gotten a look at their faces. Admittedly, the last few were nearly unrecognizable from decay, but even so I knew they weren't my mother.

So, I prodded at this thought like tonguing at a missing tooth. If she hadn't been killed by Robert Williams or his father, then she really had abandoned us. Was that better?

"I know you're fine," Dan promised. "But you still need to rest. We all do. Craig and I are heading out in the morning. We appreciate all you and your dad have done for us, but..."

I shook my head. "You don't have to explain. You guys need to be home."

"Yeah," Craig sighed. "My little girl, you know."

My stomach felt such a sharp thrust of pain that for a second I thought my appendix had burst. *How crazy would that be?* I thought. *A burst appendix at a time like this.* "I know."

Upstairs, I went to the bathroom and undressed, examining my torso in the water-stained mirror. Nothing. At least, nothing visible. I was still dirty from the woods. There were bits of twigs in the knots of my hair. I filled the clawfoot tub, trying to remember the last time I'd taken a bath. I had to have been young; in the midst of puberty, I'd decided that a number of things were too childish for me to carry on into teenagerdom, and baths were one of them.

The water was not very warm but I laid in it anyway,
curling my limbs and leaning back until I was fully
submerged. I kept my eyes open, gazing up at the bleary
amber lights through the water. I wondered if this was
how Suzette had felt, trapped under that tarp: terrified
to breathe, because if she breathed, she might then *stop*
breathing. I wondered if this was how she saw the light,
distant and smeared, unable to tell if it was sunlight or
something less real. I wondered if she still felt the pain
from the wound in her jaw, or just the lack of it.

I didn't realize I'd fallen asleep until I slammed back
into consciousness, my body lurching out of the water
with a gasp, waves of it cresting over the lip of the tub to
spill muddy puddles across the floor. Sometimes survival is
violent.

❧

IN THE MORNING, I woke to find Abby watching me.
She sat cross-legged on the floor, pulling bits of yarn
from the carpet. She'd seen my eyes open, so there was
no pretending I was asleep in hopes that she'd leave.
"You made the bathroom dirty," she said. There was no
accusation to her words; she was simply stating a fact. I
had made the bathroom dirty, too exhausted to bother
mopping up the brown water I'd spilled across the floor, or
carrying my muddy clothes down to the washer. Still, I felt
defensive.

"I'm a grown up," I told her. "Being a grown up means
you can make a mess sometimes."

Abby didn't seem to buy it. "You've been asleep for a
really long time."

I consulted my phone with a frown, and found it
clinging to its last bit of battery. I'd been in bed for over
twenty-four hours. "I was really tired."

Abby was unimpressed. She looked around my room with an interest I couldn't understand. Surely she'd been in here many times. When I was a child, there were few pastimes I enjoyed more than putting my hands on other people's things. I loved to rifle through my parents' closet and my brother's drawers in search of anything that snagged my interest. Those things I would take and hoard, a thief in my own house, a magpie curating a nest of stolen, shiny curiosities.

Once, memorably, I had gone through my mother's jewelry box and taken a small brooch. A cameo, the silhouette of a woman with elegant hair. It was just cheap plastic meant to resemble ivory, but I fell in love with it instantly and stuffed it into my pocket. My mother found it, ruined, in the washing machine the next day. That was the first time my mother hit me. After that, I took better care not to get caught.

Abby was gazing at my childhood trinkets with a hunger I found familiar. Her gaze landed on the tin can with its cherry red string. She pulled it from the dresser. "What's this?"

"It's a can telephone," I said. "I made it when I was your age. To talk to my mother."

"Daddy said he doesn't have a mother."

"We don't. But we used to, and I wanted to talk to her because I missed her."

"You talked to her with this?"

"Yes." It wasn't precisely a lie, I thought to myself. I *did* talk to her with the can. She just never talked back.

"Can I use it to talk to my mom?"

Here, I hesitated. Once, briefly, when I still entertained thoughts on the subject of children, I'd resolved to myself that I would never lie to a child just because it was easier than explaining the truth. "Sure," I decided. "She might not say anything, though."

"Did your mother ever say anything?"

"No."

Abby considered this, looking down at the can. She nodded once, very business-like. "Alright. I'm still going to try it."

"Fair enough." I stretched and caught sight of a mug of coffee on my nightstand, brown sugar around the rim. I sat up and grasped it with relief. It had gone cold while I slept, so I gulped it down.

"Aunt Bethany says coffee stunts your growth," Abby informed me.

I took another sip and wondered if I'd been a know-it-all as a kid. I feel like most kids are know-it-alls, desperate to share the small wealth of knowledge they collect like loose change from the couch. Craig's daughter, when I met her, had just done a report on dolphins for school. She spent the whole dinner regaling us with facts about dolphins: what they ate, where they lived, how they died. Dolphins, I now know, can commit suicide.

"Then it's a good thing I'm already done growing. Where's your grandpa?"

"Feeding the goats," said Abby, with a tone that made clear she did not think well of the goats.

Downstairs, I found Dan and Craig filling their tumblers with fresh coffee, dressed and packed for the road. They'd stayed behind so we could have a proper goodbye, too kind to wake me. Apparently, my cousins had taken it upon themselves to show my drivers around the town, such as it was. I asked how they liked it.

"It's nice," said Dan. "The nature, and everything. Getting away from it all."

People always say that, when talking about the country. They call it *getting away*. Like the cities are chasing after them, knife in hand, and they've just narrowly been saved by the cornfields. City people think of rural people as part of the scenery, like the hay bales and livestock. They say going out into the country is *getting away from it all* because, to them, cities contain everything. Anything outside the city is just backdrop. A nice escape from real life.

"Everyone was giving us the eyes," said Craig. "Like 'oh, there go those city-folk who caught our serial killer.' I don't think they like us very much."

I didn't have the heart to point out that, serial killer or not, everyone would probably have stared at Craig anyway. Northerners like to pretend that, because their great-grandpas are buried out in Union lots, there's no prejudice to be found above the Mason-Dixon line. But of course that's not true: just like with the Williamses, they simply don't want to admit it. There weren't a lot of transplants in places like Archer. The people who lived there were born there and planned to die there. If by chance they ever left, they'd still probably find their way back, like salmon returning to their birthplace to spawn. And old waters carried old grudges, old suspicions, and old schools of thought. I was glad my cousins hadn't left my drivers alone at all.

Now that I was finally awake to see them off, David had agreed to take them back to Rochester, where they could each rent a car and drive to their own cities.

The Monroe County prison was just outside of Rochester proper. "I'll come with you," I told David. "I want to visit Zed."

David didn't comment, but his eyebrows told me what he thought of this plan.

"Who's Zed?" asked Craig.

"My brother," I said. "He's in jail for manslaughter."

"You guys close?"

"Not lately." My dad walked in, scraping the mud from his work boots. "I'm gonna go with the guys," I told him. "To see Zed."

My dad paused. "You have to call ahead to make sure you're on the list."

"Do you go see him?"

"Not for a while," he admitted. "He took me and Abby off the list."

"Probably doesn't want his little girl to see him like that," said Dan. He had mentioned once, very briefly, a son and a daughter that he wasn't allowed to visit. I don't know how old they are, or why their mother took them away, though I suspect it had something to do with the bullets tattooed on the back of his neck. Four of them in a straight line. It doesn't take a detective to work out what ink like that means.

David dropped Dan and Craig off at the rental store. We promised to stay in touch and keep each other updated about the case. They both offered to take me with them. I waved them off. I'd already run from Archer once.

The jail looked the same as it did the first and last time I'd gone to see my brother, at the beginning of his incarceration, when we still expected a quick release. Abby had been just three and she, my dad, and I had all gone in together to sit with him at a wooden table and play cards. This was before we realized that without the money to buy him a reduced sentence, the jail didn't much care to let a source of free labor go so easily. It was owned and operated by the same tech company that owned and operated most of Rochester.

Sometime in the late 90s, Rochester had become the Northeast's answer to Silicon Valley, on account of everything being cheaper there than in New York City. IT companies flooded the market, buying out Xerox and Kodak shares easily and waging a bidding war that lasted almost a decade, until Nitonic—a hydra conglomerate with a hundred little brands like heads that produce everything from smart TVs to insulin—won the lot. They chartered and renovated the police stations, fire stations, hospitals, and schools. They opened up grocery stores under three different brands—one catering to

the all-organic crowd, one to the low-income, and one
nestled comfortably in the middle. They auctioned
off sponsorships to send low-income kids to the three
universities, with the understanding that upon graduation,
each sponsored student would be contractually obligated
to work for Nitonic for eight years. A few years ago,
Nitonic took out every water fountain in the city and
replaced them with small machines run by an app called
RFL; for a monthly subscription, you can refill your water
bottle. Every business in Rochester was either owned by
Nitonic or rented a building owned by them. Including the
jail.

The prisoners spent their days making components
for energy-efficient lightbulbs—branded Ethical Bulbs
because they use less electricity, proudly announcing
"American Made!" on the packaging—and lithium
batteries, for roughly three cents an hour. The prisoners
were charged fifteen dollars a day for room and board.
Once their sentence was finished, each of them received
an invoice detailing how much they owed Nitonic.
They were then offered a position at one of Nitonic's
warehouses, where they could work off the debt without
interest. Almost everyone took the job. How could they
say no? By the time they've finished serving their sentence,
they're used to it.

Now I called ahead from the parking lot. The jail itself
was a minimum-security facility, and I got in with little
fuss. David agreed to meander around the city for a little
while—apparently there was a fishing gear store he was
interested in—and then swing by to pick me up.

The visiting room hadn't changed much either, still
filled with round wooden tables where inmates and their
families might sit and pretend they were anywhere else.
Zed sat in his gray jumpsuit, dark hair long and curly,
beard trimmed, hands crossed in the unconscious motion
of someone used to being handcuffed.

His knuckles were bruised and swollen, which I put down as only slightly worrying. If he was in any real trouble, he probably wouldn't be allowed visitors.

"What's up, sis," he greeted. "Long time no see."

"A man tried to kill my drivers two days ago. Our truck went over the guardrail. His name was Robert Williams. He was from Archer. They're calling him the Southern Tier Strangler."

"Well hullo to you too," Zed said mildly. "And this sudden near-death experience made you want to visit your big brother, rotting away in his cell?"

"You don't look rotten to me. You'll be out in four years, if you don't do anything drastic."

"Four years," Zed echoed. "I'm glad you're not dead. Why'd he want to kill you?"

"I don't know. Yesterday I found five dead women buried behind his old trailer."

"Lord, Debbie," Zed swore. He looked at me closely. "You sure you're okay? Shouldn't you be talking to a shrink about all this?"

"Suzette Parker was the sixth woman he'd buried," I continued. "She was still alive. You remember Suzette. She had hair like Shirley Temple. Everyone called her Suzie Q."

"Sure," said Zed. "Sure I do. Thanks for telling me, I'll send her a get well card."

"What do you remember about Mom's disappearance?"

Zed's focus became ice-sharp. "Why? You find her in that hole, too?"

"No," I said. "But she was his type. Blonde, white, pretty. About my age. He killed a woman in Bath, too. Dad said she called from a motel in Bath."

"She did. Dad and I drove out there to look for her."

"You what?"

"The day after the phone call. David was still a toddler and you were obsessed with him, so we just left you with Bethany and took off. Dad told me we were on a scavenger hunt. We drove all around that city, visited every motel he could find in the phone book. He had me on the lookout for any blue cars I could see. We stayed at one of the pay by the hour places and then drove home the next day. I didn't realize till later it was her we were looking for."

I stared at my brother, who began picking at his fingernails with a forced nonchalance. I didn't remember this impromptu trip, but then I would have barely been nine at the time, and I didn't remember much from my childhood to begin with. Zed would have just turned twelve. "You couldn't find her?"

He rolled his eyes. "That doesn't mean she was nabbed by some serial killer."

"Did anyone at the motels recognize her?" I asked. "Did you ever find the car? Did Dad even report her as missing?"

"She wasn't *missing*," Zed snapped. "The bitch *left us*. You don't remember what she was like—"

"I do—"

"What she was *really* like, the shit she put us and Dad through—"

Our voices were rising, equally matched as in all things. "I do remember—"

"She was crazy," Zed said harshly. "She was crazy, and maybe she did love us, maybe she didn't, but eventually she just snapped. She chose to run and she chose to leave us behind. And I'm sorry about that, I know you needed a mom. Hell, I needed one too. Maybe if she'd stayed, or been less crazy, things with Liza would've been different. I don't know. Sometimes I think I married Mom's kind of crazy because that was all I knew. Cause I missed her."

"I know she wasn't the best mom," I told him. "I know she wasn't there for us, and when she was, she wasn't herself. I remember the screaming, and the rice in the cupboard, and...but this isn't about that. If she *didn't* really leave us, or if she left and planned on coming back, but was prevented...don't you want to know?"

Zed sighed, rubbing at a scab on his knuckle. "I need a cigarette."

"I thought you quit."

"I didn't quit, I just quit smoking in the house. I didn't want Abby breathing it."

I flinched, gaze sluicing away like oil on water. I focused on the grain in the table. It was false wood, compressed and then painted. I could feel him staring at me.

"You're gonna have to get used to her eventually," he said. It might have been the kindest he'd ever spoken to me.

"Why? It's not like I live with her." At his weighted silence, I added, "I'm just not a kid person."

"I know what you are," said my brother. He scrubbed a hand over his jaw. "You should go. Rec's soon."

"Do you remember what she said? When she called."

"I was asleep when she called, same as you. And Dad never told me." Zed waved the guard over, signaling the end of our visit. "It was good to see you. Don't come back," he told me. "I'll have your name taken off the list."

David came and picked me up. He was listening to some radio show about fixing cars. "Don't you get tired of thinking about that?" I asked. "You fix cars all day at work, and then work on the farm equipment when you get home. Now you listen to other guys talk about it while you're driving?"

"It's how I get better at it." He shrugged. "This episode talked about a lady whose engine started screeching when she turned the ignition. Turns out it was the Serpentine belts. I wouldn't've known what to do about that, before. Now if I ever get someone with that problem, I'll know how to fix it."

"Do you ever wish you'd left?" I wondered. "Do you ever think about leaving?"

"You ever think about coming back?"

"No," I admitted.

David hummed agreeably. "Some people're just better off where they started. Grass is plenty green out here. Why should I leave? So I can work myself to death just to live in some windowless shoebox? No thanks."

"Some of our shoeboxes have windows," I said. "But when you put it like that..." I liked my shoebox back in Baltimore, filled with my half-dead plants and the mosaics Miranda made out of broken liquor bottles. I liked it because it was mine, and because I felt like someone different when I was there. Someone worth being.

The radio dropped into static some ten miles out from Archer. We started seeing signs posed in front of splintering barns and pasture fences, proudly boasting: THIS FARM IS NOT SPONSORED. As we passed the general store—the only place with gas and groceries for miles—I noticed a white van with a blue logo painted on the side. It was new and clean enough to warrant interest. Clearly, it didn't belong there.

The sky was a blooming, dusky blue as we pulled up to my dad's house. The lights in the barn cast long shadows across the yard. I found my dad hunched over Maisy, the single cow left over from his family's dairy farming days, kept around for calves and milk. Her belly was wide with pregnancy, and he stroked her softly as she munched on some hay. Three goats and a litter of straight-tailed kittens scattered as I walked in.

"Is she due soon?"

"Any day, now," my dad said. "It'll be the first calf Abby remembers. Still haven't figured out how to tell her we're not to keep it for long."

I crossed over and laid a palm on Maisy's nose, feeling the soft velvet, the wet heat of her breath. "What are you going to do with it?"

"Bobby's always looking for good veal. It'll be bale season when it's old enough, so I'll likely get enough hay for next winter from it."

I'd spent too much time in farm country to feel any
sadness over the death of an animal. Things died; I
understood this even as a child. Maisy snuffed at my hand,
warm and at peace. This would be her third birth, and
she'd never kept a calf for more than three months. I
wondered if she knew what was coming. The loss she was
about to experience. I wondered if she ever grieved the
absence of life inside her. If she felt it the way that we do.

"What'd your brother have to say?"

"Not a lot. He said you took him to Bath, to look for mom."

My dad's hand went still, pressed against the calf in
Maisy's belly. "I did."

"Why didn't you take me too?"

He turned to me, mouth like a sinkhole. "You were
already at Bethany's. Seemed easier. I shouldn't have even
taken Zed. Should've left you kids out of it. If she'd just
been leaving me, that was one thing. But she left the two
of you, and that tore me up. I knew she was...troubled. We
tried therapy, what medication we could afford—I knew it
wasn't helping much. But I didn't think she'd leave *you*."

I kept my gaze on my hand, slid up between the cow's eyes.
I counted her long lashes. "What did she say when she called?"

"It's been nineteen years," he said softly. "Will knowing
really make much of a difference?"

"It will to me."

My dad looked at the kittens, who had now grown
brave and come to investigate my boots. "She said 'Water's
rising and I'm out of oats. Watch out for the shadow of
death. Goodnight, Jacob.'"

When I didn't speak, he said, "I could never make
much out of it. Your mom sometimes got these ideas in
her head, of what was real and what wasn't. When we
couldn't find her that next day, I figured she'd turn back
up eventually. She'd left before, in the early days, but she'd
always come back."

"You're sure that's what she said?" I pressed. I was running over every inch of my interaction with Robert Williams, searching for a hidden message, like rubbing a pen over the indentations left in paper. "About the oats?"

"Sure's sure."

"Have you ever heard the phrase 'oats pour when water rises'?"

"Can't say that I have," he said with a frown. "Though it *does* sound similar."

"Robert Williams said it the day he died." I watched the doubt flicker across my dad's face, there and gone again in one long blink.

"Bee, it's hardly a confession."

"I don't need a confession. I just need answers. I can't just wash my hands of it and move on. Not this time."

"Nothing could be done," my dad said quietly. He'd said the same thing when he called to tell me about Zed's arrest. He'd said the same thing when I was seventeen, throat sore from vomiting, sick with pain from a night I couldn't even remember.

I didn't argue with him. He gave Maisy one last pat and led the trek back to the house through the dark. Abby was just inside, coloring at the table. There were three figures on her paper, crude replications of people.

"Who's that?" I asked her.

"Grandpa, me and you." She had drawn my dad's beard like blades of grass, his head a bald circle. She had given me and herself the same wide, brown eyes.

It didn't mean anything, I knew. Lots of people have brown eyes. A nine-year-old could hardly be expected to draw like a professional; all of Abby's figures probably looked the same. And besides, we were related. Of course we had things in common.

"I saw your daddy today," I told her, ignoring the picture completely. "He misses you."

"No he doesn't," Abby said. "If he missed me, he'd tell me himself." She said it with no sadness or animosity. Just the simplicity of a fact.

"Your daddy's not the best at telling people things," my dad told her. He'd dished up three plates of spaghetti and carried them over one by one. "He got that from me." The purposeful eye contact he gave me was, I supposed, the closest to an apology I was likely to ever get.

❧

THE NEXT MORNING, Abby was in my room again.

"There's a lady with a camera outside," she said without preamble.

"What?" Groggily, I felt around for a cup of coffee but found none.

"There's a lady with a camera outside," Abby repeated. "She asked Grandpa about the man who planted those ladies."

"What did he say?"

"He didn't want to talk to her."

The idea of a reporter driving to Archer seemed laughable. They'd be unable to film anything live. The fact that they'd managed to find my dad's house at all was impressive.

"How'd you hear that?"

"I'm little," Abby shrugged. "Grownups don't notice me unless I talk."

"You're sneaky, you mean," I smiled. I'd been sneaky at her age, too. I'd loved to be places I wasn't allowed in, listening to things I wasn't supposed to hear.

Downstairs, the sound of someone stomping into the kitchen caught our attention.

"Grandpa went out to corral the ducks," Abby told me.

"I guess he's finished corralling."

Except it wasn't my dad I found in the kitchen, but Benji, helping himself to another clementine.

"Good morning to you too," I said, swiping a sticky wedge from him. He grunted. Upstate, people always spoke with as few words as possible, like they had a rationed amount and were afraid of running out. Words, for them, were a nonrenewable resource.

"News people outside," he informed me. "From Rochester. I think one might be from Binghamton."

"How many are there? Abby just mentioned the one."

"More than one," Benji said darkly. "They're camped out just off the edge of our property. They scared off all the deer this morning." This explained the scowl and the stomping.

"I didn't think news traveled that fast around here," I admitted. "Why are they even here? Shouldn't they be poking around the trailer?"

"They know that we're the ones who found it. Stupid county badges can't keep their mouths shut, I guess. They wanna interview us, and stuff."

"Shouldn't you and Abby be at school?" I asked, trying to calculate Benji's age. I knew he was a teenager. All the Archer kids had to go to the chartered school in Jameson, the next town over. There were only twenty-odd school-aged kids in Archer at any one time, so Jameson generously shouldered the extra cost, but we all knew any year could be the end of that arrangement. If it ever came down to it and the parents of Archer were forced to either pay out of pocket for their kids' schooling, or just abandon the education system and accept the fines, I wasn't sure which option they'd lean towards.

Benji gave me a look. "It's spring break."

"Right." I considered him. While my dad did have a complicated messaging system set up, he didn't actually have any internet at the house. Archer was pretty much a dead zone when it came to cell service, but if anyone would know where to go to get a signal, it'd be a high schooler. "So who do I have to bribe to get my phone to work out here?"

"You don't know?"

"Cell phones weren't really a thing when I was your age. Not like now."

"You know the old silo by the Amish mill?"

All us kids used to go out to that silo with filched batches of our parents' hoppy beer. "I do."

"Just inside. Half in, half out, kinda. That'll get you three bars. Hope that's enough."

"It's enough. Thanks. Watch Abby? I don't know where my dad went."

"Probably hiding from the cameras," Benji scowled.

I snuck out the door to the back porch, startling a gang of sunbathing cats. The ducks were still loose, waddling around the yard, honking with displeasure as I nudged them out of my way.

The silo was where I remembered it being, just a fifteen-minute trek from the house. Zed and I used to hike out there on summer nights, Nalgene bottles filled with beer in hand, skin slick with sweat. The other kids from town would be there already, camped out with stolen quilts and alcohol. The ones who lived farther away would drive and park their trucks in the field, headlights illuminating the campsite, moths fluttering towards the warmth.

An empty tin of Skoal chewing tobacco reminded me of the last party I'd attended at the silo. I'd been seventeen. Headlights, moths fluttering, the sound of rock music warbling from the speakers, the sweet smell of weed and tobacco. Someone had built up a fire and some of us were daring each other to jump over it. I drank some of Jimmy Greene's moonshine, even though I didn't like the taste.

"Come on," he'd needled, a sloppy drunk at eighteen. "Just *try* it."

I got talked into doing a lot of things I didn't want to do that way. When it was over, and my throat was numb from the burning, I had no one to blame but myself. After all, I'd said yes, hadn't I? He'd offered up the jar, but I was the one who'd swallowed, no gun to my head. I'd gone over that night so many times, and that was always the thought I returned to. I'd taken the jar. I'd laid down by the fire and closed my eyes. I'd worn the jean skirt, like an open invitation. For all I knew, I'd said yes, as well as any clumsy, drunk teenager could. I couldn't begrudge the universe for the choices I'd made. I couldn't be upset over something I didn't remember.

The place was barren now, splintering crates and aluminum cans strewn amongst the milkweed and goldenrod. As promised, my phone produced three bars when I stood just inside the silo's entrance. It wasn't enough to surf the web, but it was enough to make a phone call.

Miranda picked up on the fourth ring. "Hey kiddo," she rasped, despite there being only the two years between us. "You doing okay? Tired of fighting off bears already?"

"Not many bears come round here. Listen, I need you to do me a favor and I don't know how long this connection'll hold. Can you look something up for me?"

"Sure," said Miranda, voice growing tinny as she put me on speakerphone. "Go on."

"'Oats pour when water rises,' no punctuation." I heard the echoing taps of her acrylic nails against the phone screen as she typed it out.

"Just a bunch of recipes for steel-cut oats," said Miranda. "Is it a quote from something?"

"From Robert Williams. The man who tried to kill me. It's the last thing I ever heard him say."

"Creepy," said Miranda. "Weird and creepy. Oh, he was on the news! I meant to tell you. Apparently he was some kind of serial killer? Which you *did not* mention, by the by."

"I didn't know until after I called you," I assured her. "We found six women buried in the woods by his old house."

"*We*? You were there?"

"I was there," I confirmed. "One of the women was an old classmate of mine. She's still alive."

"Holy shit," Miranda hissed. "How fucked up was this bastard? Are you coming home now? Please say you're coming home."

I hesitated, the worry in Miranda's voice threading me with guilt. "No, I—how much do you know about my mom?"

"Not a lot. You never really talk about her. I know she left when you were little."

"Yeah, well. There may be more to that." I toed at a crumpled can of Busch Light.

"Like what?" When I didn't answer, she said "Like *what*, Bina? You think—you think this guy killed her?"

"I think he was killing women like her around the same time and place she disappeared."

Miranda swore viciously, each word thrown like a dart at the wall. "How's your dad?"

"He's...himself. Quiet. Sad, I think, a little. I think he's always avoided asking questions because he's afraid of the answer."

"And the kid?"

I shrugged, though of course she couldn't see it. "She's nine."

"This will probably fuck her up," Miranda warned.

"That's life, isn't it? We just keep finding new ways to get fucked up until we die."

"It's too early for your pessimistic nihilism bullshit," she complained. "Have you at least talked to her about what's going on?"

"What? No. I wouldn't even know what to say."

"Weren't you her age when your mom went missing?" Miranda asked pointedly. "Did anyone talk to you about what was happening?"

I scoffed, unable to even picture such a conversation.

"Definitely not."

"Don't you wish someone had?"

I wished for a lot of things at that age, but arguing with Miranda was pointless. "I hate when you're right."

"Lucky for you, it doesn't happen often." There was a smile in her voice, which in turn pulled at my own mouth.

I was still looking down, avoiding the glare of the blooming sun. As Miranda spoke, a shadow stretched and spread into my line of sight. I glanced up, startled to see a woman steadily approaching.

I cut Miranda off bluntly. "Hey, I gotta go. Thanks again. See you soon." I hung up before she could respond. It was unimaginably rude, but sometimes you're allowed to be rude to the people who love you. Or maybe it's less that you're allowed and more that you know they'll forgive you.

"Deborah Morton?" asked the woman. She was dressed smartly, with hair that had been recently treated to highlights in a salon, and a pair of high leather boots that clearly weren't made to suffer mud. Even disregarding the fact that I'd never seen her before, I would've known she didn't belong in these parts. "My name's Harriet Allman, I'm with *The Daily Court* up in Binghamton—"

"How much of that did you hear?" I asked her. This was also rude. I didn't feel as bad about it.

"Not much," admitted Harriet. "Something about your mother going missing."

'Not much' was still more than I wanted. "Why are you here?"

Harriet's shoulders squared and her face shifted into what I mentally categorized as her *journalism pose*. "Robert Williams may have been the most prolific serial killer in all of Upstate New York—"

"I don't mean in Archer," I clarified, waving a hand at the sorry remains of the silo. "Why are you *here*?"

"Getting a lay of the land."

"Yeah? Drawing up a map for later? 'X marks the spot where all the teenagers used to hang out and pretend they were older than they were'."

Harriet prodded delicately at the beer can I'd kicked earlier. "I can see that. Where do the teenagers hang out now?"

"Hell if I know. Probably in their bedrooms, on the internet."

She raised a sleek iPhone, screen glinting in the light. She looked rueful. "Also, I may have been hoping to stumble upon a signal. This really *is* back-country, huh?"

"You're definitely not in Binghamton anymore," I agreed. "Knock yourself out—you may want to talk fast, though. Who knows how long you'll have without cloud cover."

"Some of the other guys are real upset over not having wifi, but I kind of like it. Feels like I can actually breathe without getting a notification for something or other. It's nice being able to interact with that world on my own terms."

"Hm," I said, slipping past her.

"Actually," Harriet sidestepped, interrupting my path back to the house. "My phone calls can wait. Could I ask you some questions?"

I did my best to look uninteresting. "Me? Why?"

Harriet was not dissuaded; she looked *very* interested in whatever I might have to say. "You discovered the bodies on Robert Williams' property, didn't you? Including Suzette Parker?"

"That sure got over to Binghamton fast," I muttered, shouldering my way around her.

"This isn't the typical killing grounds for a serial killer," shrugged Harriet. "People are shocked, and when people are shocked, they're intrigued. They want to know everything they can." When I didn't answer, she added, "The nurses at Mercy Hill said that if she'd gone one more day before being discovered, Suzette would have died. You saved her life."

"You talked to Suzie's nurse? Did you talk to Suzie?"

"She's in a medical coma," Harriet said, clearly disappointed by this inconvenient turn of events. "Hopefully she'll be awake before the weekend."

"Well maybe you can go ask her your questions then." I began picking my way back through the overgrown field.

"Your mother went missing the same year that Robert Williams left Archer, is that correct?" Harriet called after me, skipping forward to keep up.

"You must have great hearing."

"I'm a journalist. I do my research." She looked almost offended.

I smiled grimly. "So what do you need me for?"

"I like to get all sides of a story."

"Maybe I don't want you or anyone else to get my side," I said. "It's mine. I'm not big on sharing."

"No one seems to be, around here," Harriet confessed. "It's strange—usually I can't get people to shut up about themselves, their lives, their neighborhoods. They want to be recorded, for posterity I guess. Proof that they did something. But here, I can't seem to get anyone to open their mouths in the first place."

"Places like Archer aren't too welcoming to outsiders," I explained. "They like to clean up their own messes. They definitely don't like other people showing up to poke and prod at 'em. Round here, the only thing worth keeping for posterity is the family farm."

"Well Robert Williams isn't just Archer's mess anymore," Harriet frowned. "He strangled women throughout New York, Pennsylvania, and even a few in Ohio. The whole Rust Belt was his killing grounds. People want to know why. They want to know where he came from."

"Why?" I asked. "Isn't it enough to know that it's done, now? He's dead. He'll never kill again. I understand wanting closure—hell, I want some too. But knowing where he grew up, seeing the shithole he used to live in, how will any of that help?"

"You aren't interested to know what makes a man do something like this?"

"There isn't always a real answer." I shrugged. "There isn't always an abusive parent, or a wooden swing. Some people are just bad, fucked up people, who do bad, fucked up things because they want to. No more, no less."

"Well I believe it's worth looking into," Harriet declared. "Just to be sure. I mean, how do we *know* Jack Williams wasn't abusive? Or that Robert didn't suffer some childhood tragedy that forged the necessary catalyst?"

"I'm more interested in the who than the why."

"You want to know about the women he murdered?" Harriet asked. "I have a list. Names, addresses. Where they worked, what they were wearing, where they were killed *and* where they were found. If they had any kids."

I squinted over at her, eyes stinging from the halo of sunlight that wreathed her hair, starting to frizz in the wet air. "Let me guess; you aren't gonna give up that info for free."

"Nothing's ever free," Harriet confirmed. "Answer my questions—*on* the record—and I'll answer yours."

"I could just call my friend back and have her give me the same list."

"You could. Better hop to it, then. Like you said, who knows how long it'll be before it starts to rain again, and it'll take at least a few days and a dozen pay walls for her to dig up even half the stuff I've got. But if you have that kind of time, then by all means—"

"Alright, alright," I groaned, waving off her heckling. "What do you want to know?"

"How did you know to look around the old Williams' property for bodies?"

"I didn't. Stumbled on them purely by accident, buried under a tarp. Shitty burial job, too."

Harriet was typing notes furiously into her phone as I spoke, while also trying to navigate her way through the treacherous thicket. "So why did you go out to the property at all?"

I paused, collecting my hair up into a coil on top of my head. The back of my neck was slick with sweat. "Honestly? I just wanted to get a look at the place. He'd just tried to kill my friends, had almost killed me too, and I was...curious."

"You didn't recognize him when he introduced himself to you?"

"I was *nine* when he was in Archer, last. And even then, we weren't exactly running in the same circles."

"But your mother was." Harriet looked remarkably sympathetic. She'd clearly practiced.

"Might've been," I agreed. "I don't know. My mother was a complex woman."

"Complex," Harriet echoed. "What an interesting way to describe her. Did you feel like you really knew her?"

"What nine-year-old really knows their parents?"

"Does your father think she might have been murdered, too?"

"I'm not sure what my father thinks. Maybe you should ask him."

Harriet smiled humorlessly. "I would, if I thought for a second he might answer. He wasn't exactly...forthcoming, this morning."

"You're the woman with the camera," I surmised. She didn't deny it. "You worried my niece."

"I'm sorry, I didn't mean to," she said, blatantly unapologetic. "She's a cute kid. Looks like you."

I very pointedly did not flinch, but my jaw did clench so hard a flare of pain shot through my teeth. "She's my brother's."

"Her mother is gone now too, isn't she?"

"Yeah, we've got a lot in common," I said dryly.

"Your brother was charged for her death."

"That's not a question," I said pointedly.

"That's two cases of men from Archer killing women," she continued.

"Zed isn't anything like Robert Williams," I said sharply, feeling the heat of defensive outrage rise up in my chest. It'd been years since I'd felt defensive of my brother, but it's the sort of sibling impulse that never fully goes away. "He made a mistake, sure, but what happened to Liza was an accident."

"The coroner's report listed fading bruises on her arms and neck," Harriet said mildly. "The sort of wounds consistent with long-term domestic abuse. I understand that's the main reason he was charged with voluntary manslaughter."

"She had bruises alright, but so did he. Liza and Zed were a match made in hell, but he didn't mean to *kill* her."

"What was she like?" asked Harriet. "If you don't mind me asking."

Leave it to a journalist to compare my brother to a serial killer and then politely ask me about his wife. I couldn't see what Liza had to do with writing an exposé on the history of the Southern Tier Strangler. Liza had been four years older than me, and we'd only ever really spent time together in the presence of Zed. I didn't have many fond memories of my sister-in-law. She was a violent alcoholic throughout her adulthood. She liked to get drunk and angry and pick fights with my brother, giving him bruises and deep gouges from her nails. She'd never forgiven Zed for forcing her to become a mother.

But before all that, when I was twelve and unbearably embarrassed because I'd just bled through my jeans for the first time, Liza once sat me down in the upstairs bathroom and patiently explained how to use a tampon. She'd ruffled my hair with affection. It was, I'd thought at the time, the sort of conversation I might have had with my mom.

"She was born in June," I told Harriet. "I think she was a Cancer. She was always bleaching and cutting her hair with cheap scissors."

"And your own mother?"

"I don't remember," I lied. "She left when I was pretty young. You wanna know about my first time, too?"

"If you want to talk about it," Harriet said placidly. "I won't say no."

"Nothing much to talk about. We were teenagers. We got bored. It was something to do. I'm sure you get it."

"Small town romance," she gave a knowing smile.

We'd reached the edge of my dad's property, towels flapping on the clothesline. "Now would be a great time to give me that list of yours."

"What, you're not going to invite me in for coffee?"

"Not my house," I shrugged. "Not my coffee."

"Were you born in Archer?" Harriet asked, thumbing through her phone for the list in question.

"Syracuse, actually. Where my mom's from. My dad worked as a contractor there. We moved down here when I was four."

"Why'd you move?"

"My grandma died. Dad inherited the farm."

Harriet held out her phone so I could take a picture of the list on her screen. "How'd your grandma die?"

"The usual. Heart failure. My Aunt Bethany found her on the floor. She did CPR, but she was already gone."

"No ambulance?"

"It would've taken forty-five minutes just to get here. And the ride alone costs two grand without a membership. Places like Archer, you die, you die. Nobody wears a 'do not resuscitate' bracelet, but it's understood. Resuscitation's too expensive. They'd rather just be buried."

"There are grants for people who open up free, sustainable clinics in poor areas," said Harriet. "Why doesn't anyone apply?"

"Lots of reasons. Those applications cost money, for one, and come with stipulations that most people can't meet.

And honestly, even if they didn't, Archer probably
wouldn't want one. They'd take it as a sign of defeat, like
they can't take care of their own. People in places like this
don't want to ask for help, even if they need it. Especially
if they need it."

"A lot of violent offenders come from abusive or
impoverished backgrounds," said Harriet. "Do you think
this had an impact on Robert Williams?"

"How could it not? But I meant what I said before. I
don't think there's always an answer. I don't think there's
always a moment you can look back on and say 'that's
why he did it.' I mean, there are tons of poor people. Way
more poor people than rich people, and a lot of them have
shitty parents and bad childhoods too. They don't all grow
up and kill women."

"Of course, there are always a variety of factors at
play," Harriet agreed. She gave me a hesitant smile. "I
know you're probably anxious to get home to—what was
it? Philadelphia?"

"Baltimore."

"Right. But I'd love to pick your brain a little more,
really get to hear your side of the story. Can I give you my
information?"

"Sure," I decided, feeling generous. I probably wasn't
going to go through with it, but there was no harm in
punching her number into my contacts. "Word of advice?
Don't go snooping around too much out here. People like
to shoot first."

"Ask questions later?"

"No. Just shoot." I grinned with all my teeth and then
turned, lumbering back up the hill towards the house.

On the porch where all the half-feral cats liked to lounge
about, I found Benji. His back was to me, hunched over
something in his lap. I gave into the urge to sneak up on him,
nudging my boot softly against the skin where his sweatshirt
had ridden up. He jumped, whatever was in his lap—a

magazine, it looked like—scattering as he whirled around. His eyes were too guilty for whatever I caught him at to be innocent. I glanced at the fallen magazine, sprawled out between us.

It was from the Williams trailer. One of the old bondage rags. From its water-damaged pages, a naked woman with a perm stared out at me. She was tied up with heavy looking ropes, strategically bound so her tits and shaved vagina were the focal points. Her eyes were slathered with makeup and wide with fear.

"I wasn't—" Benji swore to me, gone red as a tomato left too long in the sun. He looked fit to be sick. "I just never saw one before."

"A porno mag?" I asked, incredulous. I could remember boys half his age sneaking peeks at them behind school, smuggled from their fathers' hiding places in Transformers backpacks.

"Not like that," Benji said miserably.

"Okay, I get why you took it," I said, because I did. It was strange, and taboo, and came from the house of a serial killer. He was a teenager. Of course he took it. "But why look at it *here*?"

"I share a room with David," he explained. "And Becky's always barging in without knocking. And I didn't want my mom to catch me." He sounded like he didn't think *me* catching him was much better.

"I'm not mad," I promised him. "But you understand why that kind of stuff is bad, right?"

"Because the Strangler read it?"

"Because it probably gave him ideas." I squatted down, thumbing through the pages, each spread more vulgar and violent than the last. "When people look at stuff like this a lot, it's easier for them to see women this way. Something to be tied up. Something to be hurt. Inhuman. Get what I mean?"

Benji nodded. I handed the magazine back to him. He hesitated before taking it. "You aren't gonna throw it away?"

"You took it. You throw it away if you want." I ruffled his hair, like when he was a little kid. He'd rolled his eyes at it back then, too.

Inside, my dad was kneeling on the living room carpet, peeking under the coffee table.

"Drop your glasses?" I asked. He grinned, crooked coffee-stained teeth poking out through his beard.

"Naw. I'm in the midst of a riveting game of hide and seek."

"This is a great house for it," I mused, glancing around. My grandfather had done odd jobs around the antique auction and flea market circuits, which meant he usually carried some old armoire home to fix up in the barn. As such, the house was filled with pieces of furniture perfectly sized for a little girl to curl up in.

I tried to recall if my father had ever played hide and seek with me or Zed growing up, but couldn't. After my mother left, we were expected to entertain ourselves. And *before* she left, we'd mostly hidden for a different reason.

There was a knock at the back door, and Benji let himself in. He flushed when I caught his eye, no sign of the magazine. He looked at my dad expectantly.

"Ah, hell," said Dad, pushing himself up with a grunt. "I promised Benji I'd take him to his 4H meeting. Can you watch your—Abby?"

"Yeah, of course. Have fun." I watched them leave through the bay window, their forms blurred by the figured glass.

There was a closet under the stairs. I checked for Abby there first. Then I went through each room, looking in closets and heavy wardrobes and under beds. I didn't search too thoroughly; I figured she'd come out eventually, whenever she got bored with waiting to be found. I ended up in the kitchen, perched at the bartop and reading through the list of Robert Williams' known—and suspected—victims.

Angela in Youngstown, Ohio. Eight women in Cleveland, over the last four years. Kelsie in Sugarcreek, Pennsylvania. Three different women in Pittsburgh, and two in Harrisburg. Five women in Archer—though three of those bodies were so decayed that it was equally possible that Jack had killed them. Skylar in Corning, New York. Two Jane Does in Rochester. Kathy and Emma— sisters—in Binghamton. A different Emma in Hornell. Jane Doe in Bath, killed the year my mother went missing.

I had to give it to Harriet: her notes were detailed. There were dates and addresses, and she'd clearly organized the list by the trail she suspected Robert Williams had paved across the northeast, according to the timeline of the women's deaths. From Archer to Bath to Binghamton, swinging around to Rochester, then Hornell and Corning, towards Harrisburg. He stayed a couple of years in Pittsburgh before moving towards Ohio. Then he went *back* to Archer, for Suzette, before returning to Cleveland. Days later, he caught a ride on my truck, headed upstate once again. It didn't make a whole lot of sense, his going back and forth between Archer and Cleveland, but then there's a limited amount of sense you can expect from a serial killer. It probably made sense in his mind, and that's all that mattered.

I was marking down the address where Jane Doe was found in Bath, when a cupboard door started shaking. Maybe shaking isn't the right word. Rattling. It shifted in its frame, wood knocking against wood at intervals, like breathing. I froze, staring, willing it to go still. It wasn't just a cupboard. It was the cupboard my mother used to keep rice in.

When she had her bad days, and there were many, my mother became the wicked witch in every kid's story. She'd snatch up me or Zed, whoever was on hand, but only one at a time, never both of us. She'd cry and scream crazy things. Just the craziest things you can think of, like the world was ending. And she'd throw us in that

cupboard and lock the door. There was always uncooked
rice poured out on the floor, boxes and boxes of it, so that
any way we sat was painful. In the dark, I'd be convinced
I could feel things crawling on me; nightmarish insects
that didn't exist, some hybrid of spiders and maggots. I'd
feel them all over my skin, in my hair, wriggling up my
nose. It's amazing, the things we can convince ourselves of
when we're terrified. We'd be in the cupboard for hours,
sometimes. Once, Zed was in there a full day before she let
him out.

What you have to understand about all of this is
that my mother really loved us. She treated us badly
sometimes, but she did love us. She'd cry and apologize
and clutch us to her so hard it hurt to breathe. And then
she'd spend weeks afterwards making all our favorite foods
and taking us to see movies, even though we couldn't
really afford that at the time. Soon, we'd forget to worry
about the cupboard at all. We'd figure it was over, that she
was better now. And then she'd have another bad day.

Even back then, we knew it wasn't totally her fault. My
mother's crazy was passed down like an heirloom of rotten
fruit. My grandmother, who she never spoke to again
after leaving her house at eighteen, had hands like barbed
wire. Everywhere she touched bled. Every word she spoke
wounded. My mother, still an open sore by the time Zed
and I arrived, had inherited those hands, that tongue like
a boning knife. It's difficult, loving someone that can't
help hurting you. How much harm is forgivable when you
know it was done to them first?

Zed was old enough to hate her by the time she left.
I wasn't so lucky. For children, forgiveness is almost
involuntary. Two mothers exist in my memory—the one I
preserved as a child, and the one I remember as an adult.
They bleed and blur together like film strips melting in the
sun. I loved my mother. I hate my mother. It's impossible
to tell where one ends and the other begins.

"She loved us," I told Zed once, as if it might make a difference.

"Yeah," he said. "And we're still dealing with that."

I hadn't thought about the cupboard in years. It's easy to forget about the things that hurt you when you don't have to see them every day. And when you do have to see them every day, you learn to see around them. I couldn't just burst into tears whenever I walked into a kitchen.

Once I left Archer, I thought I would leave the cupboard as well. But that's not how it works. You have a place where you store everything bad that's ever happened to you. And as time moves on, you move on too. And you think you've left that place behind completely. But then one day you realize you haven't left it at all. It's still there, buried inside you.

I left Archer and that cupboard. But the cupboard didn't leave me.

And now here it was, looking me in the eyes, forcing me to acknowledge it, daring me to step closer. It was just a cupboard, an inanimate object. It was also not a cupboard, but a hole. The last hole I'd gone digging through had contained five dead women.

For one horrible, choking moment, I thought I was being haunted. This was not the first time I'd wondered. The farmhouse was very old, and both of my grandparents, and my dad's grandparents before them, had died in it. Once, when Zed and I were helping my father install new insulation in the living room, we found a cat skeleton in the wall. My mother was already gone by then, which I remember thinking was a good thing, because the bones would have made her sad. She'd grown up in the suburbs and so had never learned to live with death. She cried during Archer's slaughtering season, when the sound of pigs crying and cows lowing ricocheted over the hills. Buck carcasses would be strung up on porches and gutted, the smell of hides being tanned

tainting the air for weeks. "She's got a soft heart," the
neighbors would say whenever my mom flinched away
from the realities of farm living. At the time, I'm sure
they thought she felt sorry for the animals. Now, studying
the image my mother left in my memory, I think she was
scared. She loved ghosts and ghost stories, but she feared
what led to them. Sometimes the things that we love scare us.

My mother had a deep and abiding belief in ghosts, so
I couldn't help but believe in them too, growing up. And
didnn't all children think their house was haunted? The
ghosts weren't necessarily malicious. Often, they were
simply there, living a lonely existence, reaching out, saying
can you see me? I'm right here.

Just like us.

The cupboard continued to pulse.

I stood, every muscle in my body clenched, even my
tongue. I could feel phantom grains of rice digging
into my skin like millions of tiny teeth. I still have little
pockmark scars on my legs. When people ask, I say they're
from acne.

I circled the island slowly. I walked over to the cupboard
slowly. My socks skidded over the brick floor as I dragged
my feet. The cupboard door kept knocking, the timing
never stuttering, like a metronome. Without thinking, my
steps began to match the beat. *Knock.* Step. *Knock.* Step.

Finally, I was less than a foot away. I crouched down
until I was level with it. I reached for the handle; my
mother's lock was long gone by now.

I wrenched the door open so hard its hinges screeched
in protest, slamming loudly against the cupboard next
door. Abby stared out at me, startled. She gave a small
gasp. I pulled her out.

"What are you doing?" I demanded.

She did not cry, waterless eyes blinking back at me,
undaunted. "Playing hide and seek. I think Grandpa
forgot about me."

My hands still gripped her by the shoulders. I let go,
holding onto my knees instead. "He didn't forget. He had
to take Benji somewhere. I tried to find you, but you hid
too well."

"That's why I was knocking," she explained. "I wanted
to be found."

"You must be a really good hider," I offered, trying to
rein in my pulse. I looked inside the cupboard. There was
no rice scattered on the floor like a bed of knives. Boxes
of old pasta shells and cans of tomato soup collected dust
on the shelves. Just a cupboard, after all. I swung the door
closed again.

"No," Abby said. "People just don't know how to look."

I sent her off to play upstairs and returned to Harriet's
notes. My dad still had an old Southern Tier phone book,
tucked on the bottom shelf of a pine end table. I flipped
through the hospitality section, comparing each Bath
location to the address where Jane Doe was found.

Three pages in, I found it. Dawn Inn & Suites, an
extended stay motel.

My father was not a sentimental man, but he was
practical. Packing up my mother's belongings to save
space had made sense, but getting rid of all the reminders
she'd left behind had never crossed his mind. So it was
easy for me to find a picture of her, taken when I was very
young, still in its frame on the wall.

I had no idea how long the 4H meeting was set to run,
so when six o'clock came around and my dad wasn't back
yet, I made Abby and me some grilled cheese sandwiches.
She wanted to talk about the lady with the camera, so I
told her what I knew: that her name was Harriet and she
was from Binghamton, which was a city north of us, and
she was writing a story about a very bad man.

"Does it have a happy ending?" Abby asked. She had
ketchup in the corners of her mouth and I was fighting
the urge to reach across the table and wipe her clean.

Could a serial killer getting shot in the head constitute a happy ending? "Sort of," I told her. "Sometimes endings are both happy and unhappy."

"Are you going to live with us now?"

"No. I live in Baltimore."

"Is Baltimore near Albany?" asked Abby, for whom Albany was very far. She had gone there on a school field trip, to a special showing of *The Nutcracker*. She'd just spent a good deal of the afternoon showing me the various ballet moves she knew, about half of which I suspected were not real.

"No. Baltimore's in another state. Maryland. Do you know where Maryland is?"

She nodded. "By Pennsylvania."

It wasn't incorrect. I collected up our dishes and left them to soak in the sink.

"It's bath night," Abby told me.

"Alright."

"Grandpa doesn't let me run the bath on my own."

This didn't seem like my dad, someone who had treated fatherhood with a generally laissez-faire attitude. Maybe he figured he had to be involved now, since Abby didn't have an older brother. I followed her upstairs to the bathroom and ran her a bath. There was a colorful ball of baking soda under the sink that dissolved and turned the water lavender.

After watching Abby undress and settle into the bathtub, I turned to leave.

"You can't *go*," Abby said, incredulously.

"I'll leave the door open. Don't you want some privacy?"

Abby shook her head, watching me with wide eyes. I went over and sat on the toilet. "Your daddy used to sit in here with me when I took a bath and tell me stories."

"What kind of stories?"

Mostly the plots of his favorite action films. "Oh, lots of different stories. Do you want to hear one?"

She nodded, and I recounted what I could remember of
The Last Unicorn, which had been my favorite movie when I
was her age.

Abby reached for the bottle of discount shampoo and
held it out to me. I tried to remember if I had ever washed
someone else's hair. I hadn't. Curling one hand protectively
over her eyes, I combed the soap through her auburn curls.

"Did your mother ever wash your hair?" asked Abby.

"I think so, when I was really little. But I don't really
remember."

"Do you miss her?"

I tilted her head back to rinse her hair, massaging her
downy scalp. Everything about her was soft, like overripe
fruit. "Sometimes. Do you miss your mom?"

"Sort of. But it's hard," Abby said.

"Why is it hard?"

"I don't know what to miss."

When I could squeeze her curls without seeing suds,
I pulled her out of the water. She wrapped herself in a
towel while I drained the tub, and then led me by the
hand to her bedroom, which had once belonged to Zed.

The walls were still his favorite shade of bloody red, but
his Green Day and Metallica posters had been discarded.
Most of the furniture was the same, with the added
touches that made it clear a little girl now lived there: a
night light shaped like a cupcake; a purple bean bag chair
in the corner of the room; a shaggy green area rug. She'd
drawn a smiling sun wearing sunglasses in yellow marker
on her window.

Abby had inherited her parents' bed, which was much
too large for her. Once dried off and dressed, she settled in
the middle of the mattress, looking at me expectantly.

I gestured to the stack of books that sat on her shelf.
"Did you want me to read you one?"

Abby nodded and I picked up the topmost one. *The Little
Prince*.

"My mom and I used to read this," I told her, scooting up on the bed. It appeared to be the same copy, a little worse for wear since the last time I'd read it. I hadn't touched it after my mother left.

This book was a condensed version of the story, meant for younger kids. I read through the whole thing aloud, only to find the last three pages were missing. I frowned, running a finger over the saw-toothed edges where they'd been ripped out of the binding.

"You have to make up the ending," Abby said, unbothered. "I like it, because that means it's different every time. Grandpa doesn't remember the *real* ending." She looked up at me shrewdly. "Do you?"

I did, vaguely. The little prince died, or returned to his distant planet, and the pilot went back to civilization. I didn't remember it being overtly sad, but I wasn't sure how to explain it properly. "The prince and his rose find each other again. And even though they're both different, they like each other even better now. The sheep never eats her. The pilot goes home."

"Why doesn't the pilot go with them?"

"He can't. He has a little girl who's waiting for him at home."

Abby deemed my ending acceptable, punctuating it with a leonine yawn. "Do you have a little girl in Baltimore?" she asked muzzily. "Is that why you have to go?"

"No. You're the only little girl I've got." I put the book back with the others and smoothed back her still-wet hair.

I was still curled around her when I woke up in the morning, one arm stretched out like I meant to shield her from the ceiling's collapse. It had been some time since I'd slept in the same bed with someone else. I'm not sure I'll ever be used to the feeling of a body next to mine. Abby had rolled closer to me in the night, the wet heat of her sniffly breaths making sweat pool on my neck. Her hair was still damp around the edges. I ran the fine curls between my fingers. She stretched, pulling back to blink sleepily up at me.

"How'd you sleep?" I whispered.

"I had a dream that we rode horses," said Abby.

"You and me?"

"And Grandpa and David."

"Were they nice horses?"

"Horses aren't really nice," Abby said, with all the confidence of a little girl who fancies herself an expert on everything. "They're animals. They aren't nice or not nice."

"You really are a farm girl, huh?"

Abby gave me a shrewd look. "So are you. Grandpa says you can leave the farm, but the farm won't leave you."

In a twisted way, I supposed that was true. I'd done everything I could to leave Archer and my past behind— and then it had boarded my truck in Cleveland.

In the living room, I found a note from my dad. He'd come home sometime in the night, but early that morning one of the Amish farmers' barns had gone up in flames. The hay stored there had been too green when they baled it, and it'd spontaneously combusted. They needed someone with a car to help them transport what they could salvage, and my dad needed me to look after the kid.

The kid, that's what he called her in the note. Not *your niece*. Never *your niece*.

"Looks like you're stuck with me again today," I told her, when she came downstairs. She looked dressed for a thunderstorm. "You expecting rain?"

"I'm going to the crick," she said, mirroring that same country drawl that weighs down my dad's words.

"The one under the bridge?" I asked. "After a heavy storm, you can swim in it. Your dad and I used to catch tadpoles and race sticks and leaves over there. Mine always lost."

At this, Abby perked up, in the spirit of competition. "I'll probably beat you too," she declared, leading the way down the dirt road, kicking up little dust-devils with her yellow rubber boots.

We raced leaves and sticks and pussywillow heads and pinecones until Abby grew bored of racing. Then we headed towards the barn, where she was eager to show off the newest batch of kittens, already grown skittish and difficult to catch.

When we stepped into the unlit barn, it took a moment for my eyes to adjust to the sudden lack of sunlight. Abby was just behind my hip, so I was the first to see the trail of blood, leading from just inside the entrance towards a cluster of shadows at the back.

I shoved Abby back out the door. "Hey, why don't you go grab some of the speedy chicken grandpa keeps in the fridge? It'll be a treat for them."

Abby, disgruntled at having been pushed around, grumbled as she stomped her way to the house. I turned back to the barn, creeping slowly alongside the blood trail, eyes straining to pluck images from the darkness.

There, in the corner, sat what was left of the bodies. Five kittens, all torn apart. It could have been a fox, or a fisher. Maybe even a coyote or loose coon hound. Either way, there was no time to feel sad over the loss of life. I had to get rid of the evidence before Abby came back.

Working quickly, I stuffed the mangled bodies in an old potato sack and carried them outside, tossing them in one of my dad's metal drums meant for burning trash. Then I went back inside and kicked old straw and sawdust over the blood. I could still smell it, a hint of copper underneath stale hay and mildew, but at least there weren't big splashes of red everywhere.

I wondered if this was how Robert Williams had felt, tossing five mangled bodies into that hole. Covering them up quickly, lazily. As if he was just throwing out the trash.

When Abby came back dutifully carting the chicken, I convinced her that the kittens were out adventuring with their mama cat. We left the meat in their old rusted food bowl for them to find. I suspected the mother cat was dead too. In the animal kingdom, mothers almost never abandon their young.

We had cereal for lunch because I didn't feel like cooking. As Abby spooned one apple jack into her mouth at a time, Miranda called. I'd given her the house number in case of emergencies, since my cellphone was all but useless this far out.

"You're on the news," she said, in place of a greeting. "I mean, they aren't naming names, but they talked about how he attacked an autoline crew, and one of the drivers killed him, and then the same crew found all those bodies in his backyard."

"Wow," I joked. "I finally get my fifteen minutes of fame and they won't even say my name."

"I know you're freaking out," Miranda accused. "Don't get all flippant with me, missy. Shit's fucked up about your hometown *without* serial killer shenanigans."

"Did you just call to insult my hometown?"

"I know you hate it there," she said, growing quiet. "You're miserable just talking about it. I'm worried about you."

"I'm fine," I promised, glancing up as my dad walked in the front door. "The second I'm not fine, you'll be the first to know."

"I'll be on the first truck to come get your ass," Miranda swore. "I don't want a repeat of October."

She meant the October night six years earlier, when I tried to hang myself in my motel room. I'd just left Archer for the last time, after that ill-conceived visit to see Zed in jail. *She needs you*, my dad had said over the phone. It was the closest I'd ever heard him come to begging. So I went. The three of us played cards with Zed, stubbornly ignoring the handcuffs. We met with his lawyer, a guppy twenty-something way out of his depth. We held stilted conversation over the kitchen table. Abby was quiet and sullen the whole time. I held her only once, neither of us quite knowing what to do with our bodies. When I left, it was before daybreak. I didn't bother with goodbyes.

Along the drive back to Baltimore, I'd pulled over to spend the night at a Super 8. I don't remember taking the emergency rope from my car, or stringing it up from the ceiling fan. I don't remember hooking the noose over my head, or kicking the desk chair over with a clatter, my bat-eared next-door neighbor the only reason I survived.

When I was taken to jail—because it's illegal to attempt suicide—and interrogated, so they could determine how much of a threat I posed to myself, that's what I told them over and over: I don't remember. Apparently, when a thought or memory is too hard to handle, sometimes your mind will eat it in a form of self-defense. Then, you won't have to remember. But the echo of it will always stick around.

Miranda was the one who got a 2am phone call that night, already my emergency contact after only half a year of friendship. She borrowed a coworker's car and drove to reclaim me from Hepburn Heights, sweet-talking the doctors into an early release. I have a fuzzy memory of her hand stroking my sweaty shaved head, my voice cracking as I babbled nonsensically about things she didn't know and couldn't understand.

"I'm just like her," I told her. "I'm just like her, leaving her behind." Miranda just shushed me, like soothing a crying child. She couldn't have known what I meant. How terrified I was of my own reflection, so similar to my mom's in the grime of a motel bathroom mirror, after condemning her daughter to a motherless life.

Miranda has never asked me about my mom, or Abby. She's never even met her. But sometimes I wonder if she suspects the truth. That first night back, when I was still high and restless from the hospital meds, she curled up with me on her shitty Ikea mattress. When I pressed my mouth to hers, clumsy and wet, she only hummed and rubbed my neck. She turned her face when I tried to kiss her a second time, saying "I would in a second, babe, if I thought it would help. But this isn't what you need, right now."

She was right of course, and the kiss never came up again.

We have spent five different, better Octobers together since, but still the whole month remains tainted.

"You don't have to worry about that," I assured her. I hadn't been actively suicidal in years. Sure, most days I woke up wishing that I hadn't. But I wasn't going to actually *do* anything. "I'll be home soon."

"You'd better," said Miranda. "Love you, kid. Just—go easy on yourself, okay?"

"Sure." I hung up. My dad stood conspicuously in the kitchen doorway, letting me know he was listening in. "How'd things go with the Amish?"

"Oh, as well as they could," he shrugged a tired shoulder. He scratched at his beard. "Miranda's a nice girl."

I watched my father chew on his words like sugar cane, the visible hemming and hawing taking place in his head. "Yeah," I agreed, taking pity on him.

"You two've been living together now for what—six years?"

"Just about," I confirmed. She'd made me move in with her after the October incident. It had been difficult at first. It'd felt stifling, being looked after. I hadn't known how to let myself be loved like that. For no reason. Not because she wanted anything from me, or because we were family and she was obligated to. On purpose, just because.

"You seem real close," he mused hesitantly. Then, in a moment so out of character that I nearly laughed, he added, "You know I love you."

"Dad, Miranda and I are just friends."

"Alright," he said. "But if you *weren't*—"

"If we weren't, I'm glad to know we have your support. But as it is, we're just friends. Honest."

"Alright," he repeated. "I have to go with Bethany up to Hornell to get a new hitch put on her truck. Could you watch Abby again for me?"

"I'm starting to feel like you just want me to stick around for the free daycare."

He shrugged, unrepentant. "She's self-sufficient for the most part. You kids were always good about that. Hopefully we'll be done before she needs to go to bed."

I didn't point out that Zed and I'd had no *choice* but to be self-sufficient growing up. Dad had been off doing whatever odd jobs and menial labor he could find, dutifully scraping enough money together for us to live off of. And our mother, even when she was lucid, could barely be trusted to keep us alive. Zed had been feeding us both since he could reach the pantry's doorknob. Children raised on farms were expected to be like horses, fully-formed and already walking just minutes from the womb.

Dad sent me, armed with his chicken-scratch list, to get groceries from the only general store in town. There were just six aisles. While studying the meager selection of soup, I caught sight of Harriet rounding the corner, her highlights glinting under the fluorescent bulbs. She waved and, after I waved back, began to click over in her leather boots.

"You're on lunch duty too?" she asked amiably, as if we were old friends who'd happily bumped into each other at the store.

"Dinner, actually. What are you looking for?"

"Anything that doesn't need a stove," Harriet said, making a face. "The nearest hotel is in Corning, and believe it or not, we *don't* have a kitchenette in our news van."

"I do believe it."

She sighed, plucking a loaf of white bread and a small jar of peanut butter from the shelf. "The glamorous life of investigative journalism."

"You'd probably be better off just pitching a tent in one of the fields."

Her nose scrunched. "Don't tempt me. Hey, you know anywhere around here that's good for a drink?"

"Besides every barn big enough to hold a still?" I asked.

"There used to be a dive bar right on the edge of town, on the interstate. Popular with truckers, mostly."

"I bet they do a great martini," joked Harriet. "Well, provided it's still standing, and provided *I'm* still standing after today, you'll know where to find me if you want to get started on that story." With one last wink and flip of her hair, Harriet marched over to the cash register.

I grabbed three cans and headed after her. Just behind her in the queue stood an old, heavyset man with a shock of white hair tucked under a wide-brimmed hat. I recognized the hat before I recognized the rest of him.

The last time I'd seen Jeb Owens, I was a teenager and he was telling me how sorry he was to hear about *my situation.* My most vivid memory of him was almost identical, from eight years before. *I was sorry to hear about your mother's situation.* When something bad happens, it's always a *situation.* It's never called what it is.

I tried to imagine the man—my father's age, though he didn't look it—in his younger days, with his wheat-blond hair and the brawny figure of a man raised on his daddy's hog farm. Jeb Owens had always been burly; even in his Sunday best, you could tell he was strong enough to butcher pigs. I pictured him beside my father and the other young men of Archer, wood axes and pitchforks in hand, circling the Williamses like turkey vultures. Robert had made it out alive, but what about Jack? Had he been buried in a pit not far from the women he'd strangled? If we had investigated the dirt around that trailer a little longer, would we have found his bones next?

"Mr. Owens," I greeted, reverting suddenly into a little girl who'd just been caught tapping the mayor's maples with her brother. Some kids shoplifted bubblegum growing up; me and Zed used to steal syrup straight from the trees.

"Why, Deborah Morton," said Jeb Owens, still sounding just as mayoral as he had when I was young, murderer or not. "I hardly recognized you! You've quite grown."

"That tends to happen after ten years," I agreed.

In front of him, Harriet finished up her transaction and swung back around towards me. She approached Jeb Owens with a beatific smile and professional, outstretched hand.

"Mr. Owens, isn't it? I'm Harriet Allman, with *The Daily Court*. I understand you used to be the town mayor?"

Owens shook her hand, face slacking back into the unreadable slate of a politician. "Miss Allman," he greeted. "I was the mayor of this fine town for seventeen years."

"Seventeen, wow! I didn't even know someone *could* be mayor for that long."

"Maybe not in a big city," Owens said pleasantly. "But out here, people know who's looking out for them."

"Yes, of course," said Harriet, switching to a more sympathetic gear. "I was so sorry to hear about your sister, Kathy."

Owens cleared his throat. "Yes, well. Kathy was always a—spirited girl."

"You mean she might have gone with Mr. Williams voluntarily?"

"Well, of course," said Owens, growing defensive. "Williams was one of us. That sort of thing just doesn't happen around here. Maybe up in your fancy cities, you've got to worry about stepping into your neighbor's car. But not in Archer."

"But it happened in Archer," Harriet said, not unkindly.

"Once," argued Owens. "Just the once. Never again, now. That horrible mess is finished. Jack and now Robert are gone. Soon, another story will hit the news across the country, and we'll be left in peace. Please enjoy the rest of your stay in Archer," he told Harriet. "I'm sure it won't be long."

He turned and finally approached TJ behind the register, effectively ending the conversation.

"Well that was pleasant," said Harriet. "I can't believe he's refused every interview offer. I'd expect a politician to be more, well, political about this."

"He did *just* find his sister's body buried in a mass grave," I pointed out. "And anyway, I told you. People 'round here don't talk to outsiders. They don't like to air their dirty laundry to each other, let alone the *news*. They can't wait for all these cameras to leave."

Harriet shook her head. "You know, it's sad. If they'd just been honest with one another about the signs, most of those girls would probably still be alive. Instead they all just buried their heads in the dirt until it was too late."

"This is farm country," I said. "Burying is what they know how to do."

I pulled back into the driveway just as my dad was ready to leave, tossing him the keys to the Jeep as we passed each other on the porch. Aunt Bethany waved from her truck, idling on the curb, waiting for my dad to take the lead. Inside, Abby was drawing again. I heated up a can of lackluster chicken noodle.

That night, Abby went straight up to her room to change into pajamas, but I nabbed her by the elbow. "You want another bath tonight?"

"But it's not bath night," Abby pointed out, bewildered.

"That's okay," I assured her, somehow desperate for her to say yes. I wanted to sit with her like that again. I wanted to run my hands through her wet hair, and smell her clean head, and watch her fall asleep, warm and satisfied. "You're allowed to take a bath tonight, if you want to."

She did want to. This time, we used a ball that turned the water magenta. I sat with her as she swirled her fingers through the syrupy colors, as if she was painting. I combed and braided her hair the way Zed sometimes did for me, when I could needle him into it. I read her *The Little Prince*. I changed the ending. This time, the pilot stayed with him. Abby was asleep before I closed the book.

I didn't realize I'd fallen asleep until my dad was shaking me awake by the shoulder. Judging by the darkness, it was sometime in the middle of the night. The sound of rain staccatoed against the rooftop; an eggshell crack of lightning radiated the room in a burst of white. My dad's face looked hollowed out by the shadows, like a woodcut of a man.

"Bee, where's Abby?" he asked me. "She's not in the house."

"What?" I asked, alertness spreading through my body with a suddenness that bordered on painful. When we were teenagers, Zed once dared me to climb over an electric fence. Filled with the confidence and stupidity of youth, I did it. That's what this felt like. Being electrocuted just enough for it to hurt. The mattress beside me was bare and cold, the covers kicked off around my ankles. "Did you check the bathroom?"

Dad shook his head. "She's not in any of the other rooms either, or the porch."

"The barn?" I wondered, and he nodded his head as I scrambled from the bed.

We pulled on our muck boots in a flurry of limbs made clumsy by rushing. We didn't bother to hunt down umbrellas, just pulling a couple of rain slickers from the coat rack and heavy maglites from the shelf. I pointed out the empty space where Abby's frog-faced boots usually sat, and dad nodded again. Wherever she was, she'd pulled on her own boots to head out there. This made the barn an even likelier candidate; it wasn't too far from the house, and she may have woken from a dream and felt it necessary to check on the animals. Then the storm might have opened up, and she was still there, waiting it out.

I'd felt the simmering coils of worry since my dad first woke me up, but it didn't bloom into panic until we found the barn empty of all little girls. The animals flicked their ears and tails at us lazily, unconcerned as dad and I ran our flashlight beams over each inch of wood and dirty straw.

"I'll wake up Bethany," dad said quietly. "Get the cousins to help us search."

"I'll look over the fields," I told him, heading back out into the rain. Lightning scored the field with light every thirty seconds, the muddy ground gulping greedily at my boots with every step. I called Abby's name as loud as I could, until my throat felt like a belt sander, but I couldn't tell how far the sound carried in the storm. Fields and forests always look unwelcoming at night. Dangerous. Like prodding at a sleeping bear.

I had no idea if Abby had done this before, disappearing into a storm in the middle of the night. If it was the sort of thing Abby did, or if this was her response to the sudden road flares that had been shot into her life. Zed and I had often run off wherever and whenever we wanted, untethered and uncaring of those we left behind. No one ever came to look for us, but then again, we had never been caught missing.

I wondered if it was genetic, this urge to run. My mother. Me. Now, possibly, Abby. Ahead of me, the silo loomed, more menacing than usual in the storm. With each starburst of light, I blinked away another shard of memory from the night of the party. I really didn't remember what happened, I'd never lied about that, but every now and then I caught glimpses. I couldn't tell if they were dreams, or truth, or my mind doing its best to patch up the holes in my memory. I remembered arms gripping me under the armpits, my own legs weak like a newborn fawn's. I remembered being half-dragged, half-led into the silo, the soft grass changing to hard cement beneath my boots. I remembered wet, hot breath sour from beer. I didn't remember a face, or a voice, or the color of his eyes. I didn't remember if he asked, or if I said yes, or if it had been more of a fumbling, unspoken assumption than anything. It shouldn't upset me, I knew. It had been so long ago, and I could barely recall the night's outline. I don't think things should be able to hurt you if you can't remember them.

I tripped my way towards the silo's open mouth, shivering from the rain and adrenaline both. Archer was plenty warm during the day this time of year, but dropped easily down to forty once the sun set.

"*Abby*," I croaked, swinging my flashlight around wildly as I stepped into the metal tube. My voice ricocheted off the walls before being answered by a plaintive cough.

Abby, sounding smaller and more timid than I'd ever heard her, called back, "We're over here!"

My light snagged on her curls, a dark and matted pile of wet curls pasted to her head. She wore her boots and pajamas but no jacket, looking skinnier than usual and shaking with a worrying fierceness. She clutched one of the barn cats to her chest.

"What are you doing out here?" I demanded, shrugging my slicker off roughly and wrapping her up in it, the hem easily clearing her knees. The cat in her arms meowed, annoyed at being jostled.

"Mama cat was hurt," said Abby, teeth chattering with cold just like the rest of her. "I heard her crying, and found her out here with a busted foot. I think something attacked her."

The same something that had gotten to her kittens, no doubt. The mother had probably tried to defend them, and somehow survived. "We'll have Grandpa look at her once we get back to the house," I promised. "But we have to get you inside and warmed up. You can't just run out into the freezing rain like this. We were really scared."

Abby ducked, pressing her wet face into my stomach. "I'm sorry," she cried, words muffled against my shirt. I ran my hands up and down her arms, trying to work warmth back into her bones. Between us, the cat meowed again, followed by a smaller, more pitiful mew.

I pulled back and looked down at the sorry state of fur in Abby's arms. "What's that?"

"Her baby," said Abby, shifting the tabby in her arms

so I could glimpse the fist-sized head of a kitten. "She was laying on it to keep it warm. That's why she was crying."

So one of the babies had survived the massacre. I took the kitten carefully in both of my hands, blowing hot breaths against its shivering flank as it made its displeasure known. Outside the silo, I heard a voice call out, no doubt one of the cousins searching for me and Abby.

I stuck my head out of the silo and shouted, "Over here!" waving the beam of my flashlight around like a beacon. Aunt Bethany came running over, two umbrellas in hand. With Abby sheltered between us, we made our way across the field, towards the beckoning lights of the farmhouse.

Becky was waiting inside, stationed there in case Abby wandered back on her own, and she dutifully went out to round up the others and put an end to the search. I gave the cats over to Aunt Bethany's seasoned care, and stripped Abby there in the mud room before herding her upstairs to the bath. She shivered her way through the house and into the water, shivering still as I gradually warmed it up. I'd read somewhere that, in cases of hypothermia, sudden heat was too much of a shock to the system. It was best to warm up over time.

"I'm sorry I scared you and Grandpa," Abby said. I watched her skin slowly grow rosy with warmth.

"It's okay," I told her. It wasn't okay. I was the angriest I could remember ever feeling. Livid. Sure that I'd be hot to the touch, like the bottom of a frying pan. But I'd grown up in the shadow of a mother's constant rage, lurking like the monster beneath my bed. I could swallow mine down. I didn't want Abby to ever know that feeling.

I pictured myself putting my hands on her, just to test how deep my anger ran. Could I reach out and strike her? Leave a palm print on her skin? A bruise? Could I reach out and pinch her neck between my hands, my thumbs in the dip of her jugular? Could I scream at her, tell her all the nightmarish thoughts that had swum through my mind in that storm?

The thought made me sick, eyes closing to stave off nausea. No, I couldn't. Even now, I couldn't understand lashing out to hurt a child. I knew Zed had never spanked Abby as retribution, had never even allowed Liza to do that, too worried about where it might lead. At their most violent, they had still never raised a hand to their child. I reached for a clean towel from the basket and held it out for Abby to step into. I combed through her slick curls. I kept my hands soft. I didn't want her to ever shy from my touch, wondering if it would be kind or woundful.

She didn't shy away now, instead trailing me back into bed and curling up in my arms like a cocoon, sheltering her from the world. "If you have the urge to leave during the night again, let me know," I told her. "I'll come with you."

I felt Abby's shrewd gaze in the dark. "You'll be here?"

"I'll be here," I said. I wasn't sure if it was a lie.

"Okay," she whispered, and dropped into sleep like a tossed penny.

My father had never been a very affectionate man, but he stayed close that next day. He split his time between us and checking up on the cats, which had been set up in the mud room. The mother was too damaged to risk nursing her own kitten, so he'd taken to feeding it goat's milk from a syringe every couple of hours. Abby was delighted to play nursemaid for the cats, fetching Dad anything that he needed, trotting to and from the mud room all day.

The cousins and Aunt Bethany all swung by at some point through the afternoon, eyes tired but gruffly relieved when alighting on Abby's auburn head. They gave her one-armed hugs and ruffled her hair and shook her back and forth by the shoulders so that her head bobbed harmlessly. All of them getting a good look at her, safe and content enough, with their own eyes, feeling her with their own hands. She may not have had her parents anymore, but Abby was far from unloved and unwanted.

This thought made my leaving both easier and more difficult. Sure, I was satisfied with the knowledge that Abby was well cared for. But I felt hollowed out by the fact that the caring wasn't to be done by me.

Loving a child doesn't mean you're ready to be a mom. My mom had loved us blindingly, and scarred us just the same.

I packed my things quickly. It helped that I'd never *unpacked*. I was sitting on the sofa, looking at the framed photo of my mother, when my dad came downstairs after putting Abby to bed. He glanced at the picture in my lap and turned away.

"She'll be alright," he announced. "That storm spooked her enough I don't think she'll be running out like that again."

"At least not anytime soon," I agreed. "Did you ever file a missing person's report?"

My dad's back bowed like a tree under snow. "No."

"Why not?"

"I figured...she wanted to go. Why not let her go? I couldn't spend my life chasing after a woman who didn't want to be here." My father was a practical man, but every man had his ego.

"Did you know what she was like? Did you know…" *What she did to us* went unsaid. I had never talked about it with anyone besides Zed. I didn't know how to.

My dad sighed with his full body. Like his soul was leaking out. "I knew she was troubled," he admitted. "I knew she sometimes...wasn't herself. I knew she could be mean, and angry over anything. But I thought—most couples fight, you know. I can't remember a time my parents weren't screaming at each other like street cats. Your mother, the way she was with me, I figured she'd be better towards you kids. I didn't know how bad it was, 'til Zed told me."

"Zed told you?" I couldn't imagine him having an easier time discussing it than me.

He nodded. "That last visit to the prison, while Abby was in the bathroom. I said something without thinking, as I do, you know. He let it slip." My dad rubbed at the gnarled hair on his chin. "I never knew why she put that lock on the cupboard. I figured it was to keep the critters out. I should've known."

"She never did it in front of you," I offered.

"She did lots of things in front of me. I just didn't want to see 'em." He looked at me, his eyes permanently squinted from so many days spent in the sun. "I'm sorry, Bee. For you and your brother both."

I wasn't sure how to reconcile my knowledge of my father with the man apologizing to me. All my life I'd been waiting for an apology, an explanation. Some acknowledgement and regret. I wanted someone else to know what we'd gone through, and to feel it keenly. Now all those wants were staring me in the face, and I had no idea what to do with them. It didn't feel how I thought it would. I wasn't healed, or lightened, or grateful. I was just tired. "Can I borrow the Jeep?"

He chewed his cud and tossed me the keys. "You know when you'll be back?"

"Not really. You need it tomorrow?"

My dad's gaze strayed to my mom's photo once again, and then the packed bags sitting at my feet. He sighed. "S'pose not. You'll have to fill her up at Acorn, if you're going far."

"Okay. Is Ted's bar still around?"

He eyed me up and down. "You drinking again?" He didn't sound critical, just surprised. As far as he knew, I'd been sober since the moonshine incident.

"It's hard to stay sober when you live with a bartender. But I'm not drinking tonight," I assured him. "Just meeting a friend." I didn't know for sure that Harriet would have gone to the bar two nights in a row, but there wasn't much else to do in Archer, so it seemed a safe bet.

"Hum," said my dad. "Yeah, it's around. Over on Aspen."

"Got it." I collected my bags and the picture frame and left.

Ted's bar, which had no formal name, was a ramshackle building at the crossroads between Aspen and 49, with a sorry-looking marquee sign out front that advertised Coors Light and karaoke. A pallet board with the words "PROUD TO BE UNSPONSORED" painted across it leaned against the building's wall. I'd never actually been inside the bar; I'd spent my last year in Archer sober, and fled just before my nineteenth birthday. It was always more popular with out of towners anyway, since most locals just made their own beer.

There were a handful of cars parked outside, including two white vans displaying logos of different news organizations. The bar was sparsely packed, with a handful of groups that had sequestered themselves at different high-top tables. Some faces I recognized, some I didn't, and some clearly weren't from Archer at all. I found Harriet laughing with a couple of guys at the bar.

"Mizzz Morton," she said cheerfully. "So glad you made it! Guys, this is the girl who found *the bodies.*" She loudly whispered the last part before beaming up at me, as if we were long-lost pals. Clearly she was a friendly drunk.

"Yeah, we know Debbie," said the bartender, amused. "What's up, Morton?" It was Jimmy Greene. He gave me an awkward nod, unsure and wrong-footed around me. Most of the guys from that night at the silo weren't sure what to do with me afterwards, and it looked like the past decade hadn't changed that.

It didn't matter, in the end, that I never remembered what happened or who did it. It was enough that they'd been there. I never knew if their residual guilt was because it could have been them, or because they could have stopped it.

"Hi, Jimmy. Harriet." I didn't recognize the other two men, and assumed they were part of the news coalition.

"Damn, Morton," said one of them. "You got stacked!"

The statement itself hardly affected me; I'd been fielding comments from men about my body since I turned fourteen. The fact that this man apparently knew me did throw me off though. I squinted, trying to place him.

"That's Wally," Harriet said helpfully.

"Wally Parker?" I asked. He was Zed's age. "How's Suzette?"

Wally's smile evaporated. He took a long swig of beer. "She's still alive, and that's what matters," he said, as if reassuring himself. "Doctors said they're gonna try bringing her out of the coma tomorrow. We'll be paying the damn hospital bills—plus interest—till we die, but. It is what it is." He spoke with the bitterness of a man who knew he was too poor to be considered worth saving. I'd grown up hearing that tone of voice. He turned to face me, having to crane his neck to look around Harriet. "I never thanked you for what you did for her."

I shook my head, uncomfortable with the sudden force of his gratitude. "No need."

"There is to me," he said earnestly. "You saved Suzie's life. So thanks."

"When did she go missing?" I asked, catching him by surprise. Harriet's eyes seemed to clear instantly and hone in on me.

"Uh, well she was s'posed to be at some training event for her new job, over in Painted Post. None of us knew she was even gone till a couple badges showed up, saying they found her."

"When did she leave for the event?"

"Dunno exactly. Two weeks ago or so. Week and a half, maybe."

"Why would Robert Williams go from Cleveland to Archer, abduct your sister, go *back* to Cleveland, and then try and come back to Archer, all within two weeks?" asked Harriet, sounding drastically sober all of a sudden.

"He was crazy," said Jimmy. "Isn't that the whole point? Crazy people don't make sense."

"Plenty of crazy people make sense," argued Harriet. "And even if they don't, most of them aren't out there killing people."

"He hated women," shrugged the man I didn't know. "Probably 'cause he couldn't get any."

"He was nice enough to me," I said. The men stared at me.

"You *met* him?" asked Jimmy.

"The day he died. He was on my truck when it happened."

"*What* happened? Badges won't tell us a damn thing," Wally scowled.

"He tried to pull my driver's gun and my other driver shot him." I had recounted this story so many times by this point that it felt like making any other statement. I might as well have been talking about the weather.

The men stared at me intently. Harriet finished her beer. "You saw him *die*?"

"No. He was shot in the cab. I was in the trailer, trying not to get crushed when we flipped over the guard rail."

"Holy shit, Morton," said Jimmy. "You okay?"

Okay seemed relative. "I'm here."

"And you think he was *nice*?" asked the news guy. I think he might've held the cameras.

"I don't think he was a *nice guy*, I'm saying he didn't start swearing at me on sight. He wasn't some raging, woman-hating lunatic. He was polite to my drivers. He was polite to me. If he hadn't tried to pull that gun, we never would've known what he was."

"Ted said his generation ran him out, him and his dad, twenty years back. Everyone thought those guys were creeps," said Jimmy.

"Wait, what?" Harriet demanded. "The Williamses were *run* out of town? I thought they just left."

"They left cause we *made* 'em leave!" crowed Wally.

Jimmy scoffed. "You weren't even there. Too busy figuring out how your dick worked." He glanced at me. "No offense."

It always surprised me, what men felt was worth apologizing over. They could say anything as long as they considered it a compliment, but once talk of dicks started up, they turned into a dog with its tail between its legs and considered themselves gentlemen for it. "None taken."

"He worked the autoline route," Harriet said. She'd pulled out her phone and was consulting her notes. "Could he have been working a trip from Cleveland that took him near Archer? Suzette may have just been a convenient impulse. Then he had to work the trip home, but he wasn't finished with her so he had to come back."

"Offhand, I know of a few depots a short drive from here," I confirmed. "I don't know his autoline, so I don't know what routes he drove."

"SDF Autoline," said Harriet.

I knew a couple people who worked for them, based out of Louisville. "They stop in Corning." I didn't need to point out that Painted Post was just next door.

"She might've asked him for a ride somewhere," Wally admitted. "She rode with a coworker, so she didn't have a car there."

"Should've known better'n to come back here," said Jimmy, pouring a round of Fireball for the five of us.

"That was the point," I said, thinking back to the smugness in his voice that morning in Ohio. "He wanted to rub it in the faces of the people who threw him out."

"Why throw him out in the first place?" asked the news guy. "Why not lock him up?"

"No proof," said Jimmy. "And Ted said they were after Jack, not Robert."

"It can't have been hard to find proof if you and your cousins stumbled over a mass grave in their backyard," Harriet told me.

"I don't think they wanted proof," I admitted. "I think they considered Jack Williams their mess, and they wanted to clean it up their way."

"I couldn't find any record of Jack Williams after that summer," said Harriet. "It's like he dropped off the earth." None of us offered a response. She downed her own shot of whiskey, and then mine, which I had pointedly ignored.

Jimmy disappeared, aggressively wiping down a different section of the counter. Wally turned his attention to the bottom of his glass.

"So that's it?" asked the news guy. "That's how things go here? When someone does something bad, they're either killed or excommunicated so they can become someone else's problem?"

"Welcome to Southern Tier, Mark," sighed Harriet.

"Where are you from?" I asked him.

"Long Island."

"That explains it. You have to understand, these are people that aren't covered by the badge. And the people they hurt aren't either, so the badge doesn't care either way. And even before the privatization, places like Archer were falling through the cracks. These people, they grow up knowing no one else will ever care about them. So they stop caring about other people."

"So we're just supposed to accept that?" asked Mark. "That it's a dog eat dog world, every man for himself? I mean, then what the hell are we even here for? No one's gonna care about us if we can't even look out for each other!"

"I'm not saying they're right for it," I told him.

"But that's how it is in the *great private sector*." He frowned deeply at his own soft hands. "If we accept it, that's no better than agreeing with it." He stood from his stool, only a little unsteady, and wobbled to the bathrooms.

"He's still new," Harriet explained. "Optimistic."

"Someone's got to be." I turned to look at her. A day's worth of sweat had made her makeup smudge in the corners of her eyes, and her hair was stuck to her chin, but she didn't look even half as drunk as she had at the start. "Still interested in getting my story?"

Harriet's eyes flashed with an interest that bordered on desperate. "Of course."

"How do you feel about a road trip?"

"Depends on where you wanna go," Harriet said, though she was already jumping down from her own stool. She left forty bucks on the bar.

"Bath. The Dawn Inn & Suites."

Harriet peeked at me, cat-eyed. "Is this a closure thing?"

"It's an investigation," I said vaguely. "You're an investigative journalist, aren't you? Figured you'd want in."

We walked as we spoke, and Harriet followed me into the Jeep amiably. She made a face as we passed the marquee, gesturing at the tattered rebel flag pinned above it. "Don't they know this is a union state?"

I shrugged. "It doesn't matter where you are. If an area's mostly white and rural, you'll find that flag. If you asked any of them about it, they'd say it was a sign of freedom, not racism. 'States' rights' and all that."

"Despite the fact that the state couldn't give a damn if everyone out here dropped dead," scoffed Harriet. I shrugged again, used to the backwards logic of the backwoods. My family had carved a foundation deep enough into Archer that the rest of the town politely ignored our Jewishness, but if we were to hang up the

Magen David, or start wishing them a Happy Hanukkah, I couldn't say with confidence that they'd react well. There was a reason I'd told Miranda to stay put.

My dad had an old GPS—one of those first, clunky models—held up on his windshield with dust and spit. I keyed in the motel's address.

"I'll be honest, I didn't take you for the tell-all type," Harriet said suspiciously as I pulled onto the interstate.

"I'm not. You're not here because I want to write a book."

"Then why *am* I here? You already have the address."

"You're here because I need someone to take the car back to my dad," I admitted.

"You're not going back to Archer," Harriet realized.

I watched my hands flex on the steering wheel. On the radio, quietly, Stevie Nicks sang about a woman taken by the wind. I wondered if this was anything like the night my mother left that town, and everything in it, behind. If she'd struggled with this tangled up feeling in her chest, too. "No," I confirmed. "I'm not going back. You weren't ever really drunk, were you?"

"People tell you more if they think you're not likely to remember it in the morning."

"You're like a TV reporter," I said, shaking my head. "What are you still doing in Binghamton? Shouldn't you be in New York City writing about Wall Street conspiracies?"

"I like Binghamton," Harriet shrugged. "Not too big, not too small. It's my Goldilocks zone. What about you? You don't ever miss country living?"

"Only people who've never lived in the country can miss that," I snorted, even knowing it wasn't true. My dad had missed Archer, achingly, each year he'd spent outside it. But I'd never loved it like he does. "I like the city. I can walk by a hundred people in one day, and none of them will ever recognize me."

"That sounds lonely."

It was lonely, but I'd been lonely in Archer, too. I think I'd be lonely anywhere. "I find it comforting."

The drive to Bath was not long. Calling it a road trip may have been overzealous. We pulled into the motel parking lot just fifty minutes after leaving the bar. We stared up at the vacancy sign, illuminated orange, bleeding out at us like a split clementine.

"Do you know which room she was found in?" I asked.

Harriet shook her head. "I couldn't get much detail. Not even a morgue shot. Usually they save those in the files of victims who were never identified."

"How do you get a hold of all this stuff?"

She scoffed, flashing her wallet at me. "How else? Most cops have a flat rate for info on cold cases. Ongoing ones are a little more. Plus, Binghamton's departments are all chartered so if you have a local address, they'll let you poke around."

"Like a membership," I mused. "And if you aren't from Binghamton but you have to report a crime there?"

"It's a little harder," Harriet admitted. "There's the usual reporting fee, and then a two to three-week callback period."

"Country clubs with a badge."

"No system's perfect," said Harriet.

The kid working the motel's front desk must have been about seventeen—certainly too young to remember a random woman who'd died there nearly twenty years ago. He glanced up at us from his handheld console, incredibly disinterested in us both.

"It's sixty-three for the full night, but eleven-fifty by the hour."

Harriet and I shared a look of raised eyebrows. "The night," I decided, and the kid sighed, pausing his game before swinging over to the ancient computer.

"There was a woman who was killed here," said Harriet. "Do you know which room she was in?" At the kid's blank stare, she added, "We run a ghost-hunting podcast."

The kid resumed clicking at the screen. "I dunno about any murder, but Room 214 is supposed to be haunted."

I imagined my mother's reaction to becoming someone else's ghost story. I think she'd find it funny.

"That's perfect," Harriet smiled charmingly, taking the offered key cards.

"Don't burn anything," he warned us. I handed over my credit card. We climbed the open staircase to our room.

My job has made me something of a connoisseur of cheap motel rooms, and this one was decidedly average. I could convince myself I was staying there for an overnight, set to load up the truck and leave for Buffalo the next day. There were two beds, both full-sized and each outfitted with polyester comforters a deep burgundy that would disguise all manner of stains. Likewise, the carpet was dark and stiff in small patches. The bathroom light was the sickly yellow of fly tape. The faucet leaked.

"Not the worst place I've let someone take me from a bar," said Harriet, laying atop all the covers on her chosen bed. It was probably a smart decision to avoid the sheets. "Do you think she was here?"

"I don't know. I'm not a psychic."

I ran a finger along the bug-eyed television screen, listening to the electric crackle of static on skin. I opened all of the dresser drawers, which were splintered and empty. It probably wasn't the same dresser. Above it hung a framed photograph of a conch shell, zoomed in so closely it resembled a spiral staircase. The frame was splintered at the edges, weathered and worn down as the rest of the place.

I crossed the room and opened the single drawer of the nightstand. Inside was a King James Bible, the golden lettering on the cover nearly rubbed away from use. I pulled it out and idly flipped through the pages. The book fell open three quarters from the end, revealing an old piece of paper that had been folded inside.

It was one of the missing pages from *The Little Prince*. The last one. I could have taken it home and compared it to my old copy to be sure, but I didn't have to. I knew.

I stared at the picture, thick creases in the paper like varicose veins, sawed-off edges grown soft with age. *Please comfort me. Send me word that he has come back.* I had not cried, as a little girl, when my mother read me the ending. I cried now.

I set the Bible back in its drawer. The page I held onto. I looked up at the telephone, once white, now eggshell from age. I pictured my mother, sitting on the edge of this bed, punching in the numbers, listening for the sound of my father's voice. Her mind on fire, her words nonsensical, but desperate to get out. Desperate to reach through the phone line to him, to make him understand.

Had Robert Williams been staying next door, a tiger pacing in its cage, anxious for its next hunt? Had he heard her crying through the wall, screaming at the ghosts in her head? That phrase, her words, had they imprinted themselves on him so he couldn't help but pass them on years later? Had he knocked at her door, curtain rope in hand? Or had that come later?

The possible endings were endless. I knew too little. I knew enough. I knew my mother had been in this hotel room. I knew a woman had died here. I knew Robert Williams was finished, now. There would be no more bodies buried under that tarp. It would have to be enough.

Across the room, in the dark, Harriet's voice reached out to me. "You okay?" She sounded fuzzy, not far from sleep.

"Do you think my mom would have come back for me?" I asked her.

"Do you think she should have?" asked Harriet.

Of course, I thought, but then—*should* she have? Wasn't it a mother's duty to care for her children? What if she was a mother in name only? What if she wasn't even a mother in name?

I thought of Abby, gazing up at me with her dewy eyes, her soft form curled against me. I had never thought to want that, and now I couldn't stop. She'd fallen asleep beside me so easily, as if all she needed was to know I was there, standing guard.

"I think I have to go back for her," I told Harriet. "Even if my mother wasn't going to, I should."

Harriet didn't answer. When I looked over, I saw that she'd fallen asleep.

☙

HARRIET, IT TURNED out, was a morning person.

"I don't remember asking for a wakeup call," I grumbled when she shook me awake just after 8am. Apparently she'd been on the phone with various local clerks and secretaries since 6:30 that morning, and was flushed with three cups of bitter complementary coffee.

"I want to swing by the hospital before I hit the interstate," she explained, tossing my jeans at me, which I'd peeled off sometime in the night. "Still not coming back with me?"

I shook my head drowsily, taking the offered cup of burnt coffee and sticky artificial muffin she'd snagged from the lobby downstairs. I shuffled along after her, yawning into my breakfast. "I'll come. What hospital?"

"Saint Lucia's," she said, putting the address into the GPS. "It's a veteran's hospital. They decided to accept the Parkers' farm as collateral and transferred Suzette there because the trauma surgeon has experience with wiring jaws."

At this, I felt suddenly ice-cold and alert. "Is she awake?"

"As of five-forty-five this morning," Harriet confirmed. "She's agreed to see you."

"How did you set this all up?"

"It *is* my job," she said pointedly.

At that, I gave Harriet a shrewd look, which she ignored. "And I don't suppose she's agreed to speak to a member of the press."

"Of course not," she said primly. "I'm not going there as a journalist, I'm going as your moral support. I'll be very respectful."

"Sure," I agreed and blew gruffly at my coffee, trying to cool it down.

Saint Lucia's was not very far from the motel, and the parking lot was half empty. Harriet walked briskly up to the front desk to sign us in and retrieve Suzette's room information, looking for all the world like she did it every day. I followed along in her wake, drifting like dust on the tail of a sunbeam.

Suzette had her own room and though it was small, it was bright and sunny with one wall made of windows. She was staring through the glass when we entered. Someone had French braided her hair. Around the lower half of her face was thickly wrapped gauze. In a chair at her bedside slept an older woman I assumed to be her mother, though I didn't remember her well enough to know.

"Hello Suzette," Harriet said gently. Suzette offered a limp wave.

She couldn't speak, I realized. Harriet seemed to understand this as well. She held up her phone.

"We'd like to talk, if you don't mind. You can text your answers."

Suzette, in turn, held up a phone of her own. She typed something into the screen, and a robotic voice answered "Way ahead of you."

The wonders of the twenty-first century. Harriet and I pulled up two skinny metal chairs from across the room, avoiding the collection of flowers and teddy bears in t-shirts and slightly deflated balloons. We were careful not to wake up her mother.

"I'm Deborah Morton," I said, focusing only on the green of Suzette's eyes. "We were in school together."

Suzette typed furiously. "I remember. You were the one who found me."

"Yeah," I swallowed dryly, desperate not to think about what she'd looked like then, when I was so sure she was dead. "Do you remember anything about that day?"

"You guys are late," Suzette typed. "The cops showed up right after I woke up. I already told them everything."

"We aren't the cops," said Harriet. "Robert Williams— the man who tried to kill you—he died in front of Deborah. The day before she found you."

I watched those green eyes expand. "I knew he was dead, but they didn't tell me what happened," she typed. "Did you kill him?"

I shook my head. "A friend of mine did, in self-defense. He nearly got me killed too. And," I hesitated, clutching the fact of it to my chest, reluctant to give it up. "And he probably killed my mom. I'm pretty sure."

Suzette typed slowly. "I'm sorry. I don't remember much. Mostly I remember thinking I was dead. I think it rained a lot. The doctors think that's why I didn't die of dehydration. I wasn't really awake for most of it."

"What was he like?" asked Harriet. "Before you knew what was happening."

Suzette considered the question. "You know, I actually felt bad for him. He seemed odd, and I remembered reading about how socially awkward people are often shunned and teased by society. My first thought was to avoid him, but then I felt guilty, because you hear all the time about odd people who are perfectly nice and only deserve a chance."

"Do you remember seeing anyone else?" asked Harriet. "Any other women he was holding? Any who were still alive?"

Suzette shook her head minutely, still stiff. She turned to look out the window again before typing a response. "I remember feeling sunlight. I hadn't felt it in so long, it hurt at first. Isn't that weird? It was all I wanted while I was trapped there, and then when I finally had it, it hurt more than anything."

"It's not that weird," I assured her. I pulled out the picture of my mother. "You don't recognize her, do you?"

Another small head shake. "I'm glad he's dead," she typed.

"Aren't we all," agreed Harriet. She laid a business card down on the mattress. "If you ever want to tell your story."

I nodded my goodbyes to Suzette and dragged Harriet out of the room. "What happened to being respectful?"

"That was perfectly respectful," Harriet argued. "And don't think I've forgotten what you promised. Even if you're coming back to Archer after all, I still expect first dibs on your feature."

"It won't be that interesting," I warned her, stepping out into the sun. "What is it you want to know?"

Harriet looked at me like it should have been obvious. "Everything."

"I don't even know where to start."

"Most people start at the beginning," Harriet suggested. "Where were you when it happened? When it began? Start there."

She led the way through the parking lot and passed the car. At my confusion, she gestured at the cemetery across the street from the hospital. Apparently she'd made some calls about that, too. Jane Doe, buried in August of 1999, was exactly where the clerk said she'd be. We stared down at the barren headstone.

"Would you like to say anything?" she asked gently.

"Not really." I retrieved my mother's photo and then the torn page from *The Little Prince*. Carefully, I removed the picture frame's cardboard back, and slid the page between her face and the glass before replacing it. I set the frame down on the grave.

My mother told me once that ghosts didn't haunt their own bodies, or even necessarily where they died. She said they haunted the places they missed. I don't know if her ghost will ever stop by her nameless grave and see that frame. I don't know if she'll read the page and understand, instinctively, what it means. I have to hope it'll mean something, if only to me, and whoever the town employs to cut the cemetery grass.

We reached Archer in the late afternoon, only to be met by Becky on her way to the barn. She was sprinting through the yard haphazardly, and we narrowly avoided a collision. Harriet poked her head out the window.

"What's the big idea?" she barked.

Becky ignored her, turning a look of wide-open joy on me. "Maisy's in labor!" She took off towards the barn again.

"It's a cow," I told Harriet, who looked struck by lightning at the thought of some woman named Maisy about to give birth in a barn. "You should come help," I added. "You might actually learn something about country living."

"Oh, I think I've learned enough to fill a book," Harriet said, but followed nevertheless.

Inside, the barn was hot enough to make sweat bloom and drip under my jacket. My dad was there, and Aunt Bethany and the cousins, each doing their part to make Maisy as comfortable as possible while she brought another life into the world. The ducks and goats and surviving barn cats had been corralled somewhere else, replaced with heaps of hot, wet towels and buckets of water. Maisy mooed plaintively from her position on the hay-covered ground. My dad rubbed the bulge inside her flank, which had dropped noticeably.

"Good girl," he murmured. "You've got another one in you, I know. I know."

"Where's Abby?" I asked Aunt Bethany, who was dutifully wetting more towels.

"Out in the fields. She didn't wanna stay. I think it scared her."

Harriet was standing between Benji and Becky, looking fascinated by the procedure before her, so I snuck back into the fresh air alone. Combing the horizon for a familiar crop of auburn hair, I caught sight of her in the old plastic playset she'd inherited from Zed and me. I couldn't believe it was still standing, to tell the truth, scarred from years of harsh Northeast winters. Once, it had risen like the sun over our childhood kingdom. But, like everything else, it faded over time. We'd stopped going near it sometime after our mom left, when it got infested with brown recluses seemingly overnight and became uninhabitable.

"How come you don't want to be with Maisy?" I asked as I approached. She was curled up in the aged turquoise tower, which put her level with my shoulders.

"She sounded like she was hurt," Abby said, refusing to look at me.

"She probably is, a little. But that's why Dad and Aunt Bethany are helping her. So she isn't hurt too badly."

"Benji said she's been a mother before."

"She has."

"Then where do her babies go?" Abby asked.

"They go to another farmer, who needs a baby cow. Dad doesn't need more than one cow, so he just keeps Maisy."

"Shouldn't babies stay with their mothers?"

"Boy," I said dryly, heaving myself up onto the platform beside her. "You sure aren't making this easy on me, kid. Sometimes, it isn't best for the mommies and babies to stay together. Sometimes one of them needs to go somewhere else, so they have to be apart."

"Like how you need to go to Baltimore?"

I reached out and brushed a hand through the snarls in her curls. I couldn't seem to stop touching her, now that I finally could. I wanted to lay my ear against her chest and hear her heart beating. She was so small when she was born—nearly a month premature. The doula hadn't said anything, but I could tell she'd been worried. I'd seen Maisy's mother give birth by then, and that was all I could think of at the time, sitting in the bathtub upstairs, wet with bodily fluids I couldn't even name. I kept thinking about that calf, sliding out of her mother like it was the easiest thing in the world. Abby was easy like that too.

When she was first laid in the crook of my tired arms, body all wrinkly and disgusting from birth, I'd thought, *Maybe I can actually do this*. I'd thought about my own mother, and what her first words to me might have been. If she'd known, even then, that she wasn't meant to keep me.

"I might not need to go to Baltimore, actually. Not for a little while yet," I said, watching her eyes squint and then swell as she put two and two together. She leaned against me, ever so slightly, just enough so I could feel her warmth.

My mother used to take naps in the sun, nearly every afternoon that was dry enough. She'd spread a quilt over the grass outside, in the sunniest patch she could find, and sleep there for thirty minutes at a time. Once when I was very small, I remembered toddling up to her, splayed out in the yard. She looked at me warily, tired, always tired. She thought I was there to disturb her rest, which I was very good at doing.

But instead I'd just flopped down beside her, curled up at her side like a cub to its mother's belly. I fell asleep without hesitation. I hadn't even been tired. I'd simply wanted to be near her, because I loved her, and I trusted her to look after me as I slept.

I turned this memory over in my mind as Abby's breathing evened out where she'd slumped down beside me, head pillowed on my lap. I combed the curls from her face, gentle enough not to wake her, keeping watch. Across the field, somewhere in the woods, a coyote began to howl.

ABOUT THE AUTHOR

Joan Tierney is a part-time writer, part-time wanderer, and full-time cat mom. When she isn't flying, she can be found in Virginia.

ABOUT THE PRESS

Neon Hemlock is a Washington, DC-based small press publishing speculative fiction, rad zines and queer chapbooks. We punctuate our titles with oracle decks, occult ephemera and literary candles. Publishers Weekly once called us "the apex of queer speculative fiction publishing" and we're still beaming. Learn more about us at neonhemlock.com and on Twitter at @neonhemlock.